I0667146

ARTISTIC APPEAL

ANDREW GREY

Dreamspinner Press

Published by
Dreamspinner Press
4760 Preston Road
Suite 244-149
Frisco, TX 75034
http://www.dreamspinnerpress.com/

Cover Art by Anne Cain   annecain.art@gmail.com
Cover Design by Mara McKennen

ISBN: 978-1-61372-127-8

Printed in the United States of America
First Edition
October 2011

eBook edition available
eBook ISBN: 978-1-61372-128-5

Readers love ANDREW GREY

A Serving of Love

"…delightful characters to root for and a romance that will leave you aching for more."
—Love Romances & More

Love Means… No Fear

"I would recommend this story to anyone looking for romance. I also found this series to be a lovely introduction to m/m erotica."
—The Romance Studio

Accompanied by a Waltz

"A story about first love, loss, and the rediscovery of love all wrapped up in its pages."
—Fallen Angel Reviews

A Troubled Range

"…Andrew Grey delivers a solid, sweetly romantic, and delightful story that will leave you clamoring for more after the last page is read."
— Love Romances & More

The Best Revenge

"…one of the most romantic and heartwarming stories I've read."
—Man Oh Man Reviews

http://www.dreamspinnerpress.com

To Mom and Dad

CHAPTER 1

BRIAN arrived home from the office later than usual, thankful that day was behind him. "Zoe," he called, and he heard footsteps scurry along the upstairs hallway before clambering down the stairs, the sound reverberating through the small, old house.

"Daddy," she squealed as she jumped into his arms, and Brian twirled her around as he hugged his daughter to peals of laughter. "I got an A in math today, and I learned how to spell M-I-S-S-I-S-S-I-P-P-I." She sang as she spelled, and Brian smiled as he listened before twirling her again.

"Where's Aunt Georgia?" Brian asked.

"She's upstairs playing Mario Kart. You can play too," Zoe told him, and Brian set her down, following her upstairs as she dragged him by the hand. As he got closer to Zoe's playroom, he heard the sounds of engines and crashes followed by quiet swearing.

"Georgia, please don't swear around Zoe," Brian said as he entered the room where his younger sister was holding a plastic steering wheel, frantically turning it and pushing buttons while she swore under her breath.

"It's okay, Daddy," Zoe cried as she jumped onto the sofa, "I know I shouldn't say words like shit, fuck, and ass." Brian watched as it took Zoe a second before she realized those words had crossed her lips, and then her hands clamped over her mouth and she stared at Brian.

Brian glared at his daughter and then at his sister, who at least had the grace to put down the game controller and look appalled. "I'll deal with both of you later," he growled before walking into the bathroom and closing the door, and then bursting into laughter. Brian held his sides as he tried not to make too much noise and give himself away, but he just couldn't help it. It took him a few minutes to get himself under control. After using the facilities, he washed his hands and opened the bathroom door. The house seemed quiet, the whirr of the game silent. Walking into the playroom, he saw Zoe sitting on the sofa with his Georgia next to her. They were reading together, looking angelic. Brian wasn't fooled for a second. "Zoe."

"I'm sorry, Daddy," she said, running into his arms. "I didn't mean to really say those words."

"I know," he said, glaring at his sister, "and if someone didn't swear like a sailor, you wouldn't have heard them."

Georgia rolled her eyes, but had the decency to at least look contrite. "Gerald from your office called just before you got home to remind you about the party tomorrow night, and he said to tell you to stop by early."

"Kimmy called too," Zoe told him, squirming to get down. "She asked if I could stay the night tomorrow. Can I pleeease?" She jumped up and down to show her extra-special excitement.

"Do you want to go to Kimmy's or to see Uncle Gerald and Uncle Dieter? Remember that tomorrow is their Christmas party. This year they even sent you your own invitation in the mail," Brian reminded her and waited for her answer.

"Can I go to Kimmy's on Sunday?"

"If her mother says it's all right," Brian answered, pleased with his daughter's choice.

"I'll call and find out." Zoe was gone and down the stairs before Brian could tell her to wait until after dinner. Giving up on that front, he turned to Georgia.

"I know, I know," she said, trying to diffuse the situation. "You don't have to lecture me. Mom does that plenty."

"Then stop acting like you need to be lectured. Zoe adores you and hangs on every word you say. When you're not here it's 'Aunt Georgia' this and 'Aunt Georgia says' that. She listens and she watches everything. For example, she told me about seeing you kissing another girl after you left last night." Brian sat on the sofa next to her and watched as Georgia bristled like a porcupine. "Now, before you get all bent out of shape, I explained to her that some girls like boys and some girls like other girls, just like some boys like other boys. Do you know what she asked me?" Georgia shook her head. "She asked, 'Is Aunt Georgia a lesbian?'"

"What did you say?" she asked, her arms folded defiantly over her chest.

"I didn't say anything, because I didn't know. Are you?"

"Mom will freak," Georgia answered. "Are you gonna freak too?"

Brian wouldn't be put off and used his lawyerly court voice. "Just answer my question."

"Good God," Georgia responded, rolling her eyes. "Yes, okay, I'm a lesbian. That's enough of the third degree. I'm going home so Mom can give me grief about the fact that I'm not engaged yet." Georgia stomped toward the door.

"Hey," Brian said, a little more sharply than he meant, and then he softened his tone. "You need to be who you are, not what Mom wants you to be."

"You mean you're not going to give me shit, I mean crap, about it?" She actually seemed shocked.

"Hardly." Brian looked around, listening for Zoe, but heard nothing. "Glass houses and all that," he responded.

"What does that mean? Mom doesn't blame you for the divorce. Barbara the bitch was the one who cheated."

"This has nothing to do with her," Brian said, wondering why he was defending his ex-wife. He could simply let Georgia think that was it. "I married her because she was pregnant with Zoe. I was young and thought it was the right thing to do." Brian was interrupted by Zoe's footsteps banging on the stairs. For a little girl, she made more noise than anyone Brian had ever heard.

"Kimmy's mom said Sunday was okay," Zoe pronounced happily, and Brian made a mental note to call her as Zoe jumped on the sofa.

"We don't put our feet on the furniture," Brian reminded her, and she slid down.

"Uncle Dieter called, and I asked him if he was going to have the candy-cane tree this year, and he said yes." She jumped off the sofa before throwing herself into his arms. "He also said to tell you that they have someone they would like you to meet." Zoe gave him a hug and then got down, powering up her Wii. Brian tried to shake off Dieter's message, but he could still feel a flutter of excitement inside. When he looked at Georgia, she had an "Oh my God" look on her face, and then she smiled and nodded slowly.

"I have to go," she told him before hugging him tightly. "Have fun tomorrow," she said and then whispered in his ear, "I get the feeling this isn't a girl they want you to meet." Georgia looked him in the eye for a second before she smiled and hugged him again. "Mom is going to shit a cow."

Georgia jumped back and laughed as she hurried downstairs, and Brian heard her call her good-byes, then the front door closed. "I'm hungry," Zoe pronounced without looking up from her game.

"Then put everything away, put your shoes on, and shut down your game, and we'll go out for dinner," Brian told her, and she nodded, but continued playing. "Zoe, I could always cook."

Zoe looked at him like he'd just scratched the needle over a record. The game was turned off and the controller put away, and she suddenly became a tornado, cleaning up her toys. Then she bounded into her room to put on her shoes and socks. Brian walked to his bedroom to change his clothes. By the time he walked down the stairs, Zoe was waiting for him—they both knew his cooking was terrible. Turning off the lights, Brian locked the house and they headed for the car.

"ZOE, are you ready to go to the party?" Brian asked as he pulled on what he hoped was a nice sweater. The one thing that Barbara had always had was good taste in clothes, and she'd always made sure he looked appropriate for every occasion. But since their divorce, he'd sort of been winging it, and sometimes not very successfully.

"Yes," Zoe said from the door to his bedroom. He looked at her and she began to giggle. "You look funny, Daddy."

"Why?" He looked down at himself. Plain shirt, dark dress slacks, nice sweater that didn't look out of place.

"Your socks," she said, giggling, and he lifted his pant legs, realizing he'd left on the white socks from earlier in the day. Hurrying, he toed off his shoes and replaced the white with black socks.

"Better?"

Zoe nodded her head, and Brian held out his hand. After turning out the light, they headed downstairs together as the phone began to ring. Brian debated answering it, but did so anyway. He regretted it as soon as he did.

"Brian." She sounded rushed.

"Hello, Barbara." She had wonderful timing, if nothing else.

"I'll be picking Zoe up tomorrow morning first thing," his ex-wife commanded.

"No, you won't. She's going to Kimmy's tomorrow, and we have plans in the evening," Brian explained levelly.

"But it's my weekend, and I want to see her." Barbara only ever wanted to see Zoe when it was convenient for her.

"Last weekend was your weekend, but you asked me to take her because you were going out of town with what's-his-name. This is my weekend, and you will have her again next weekend," Brian responded firmly as he watched the excitement flow out of Zoe, his daughter moving closer to one of the walls for support. "She's made plans for tomorrow, and I'm not disappointing her."

"I'll get my lawyer to call the judge," she threatened, and Brian stifled a laugh.

"Please do," he retorted before placing his hand over the phone. "Zoe, go upstairs while I talk to your mother for a few minutes. And don't worry, I'm not letting her change your plans for tomorrow." He tried to be pleasant to Zoe even as he seethed at her mother. Slowly, Zoe climbed the stairs, and Brian returned to Barbara. "Now you listen," he said once Zoe was out of earshot. "I have kept track of every changed visitation, every time you've complained that you couldn't take Zoe for whatever reason, and I will use that plus your whoring around against you. Remember, you already lost joint custody. Keep it up, and next I'll request supervised visitation."

The scream he got through the phone would peel wallpaper. "You wouldn't!"

"As I said, you have Zoe next weekend. I'll call you during the week to make arrangements. Now, we have a party this evening, and she's going to Kimmy's tomorrow. Good-bye, Barbara." Brian hung up the phone, wondering, not for the first time, how he'd managed to stay married to her for so long and why he hadn't realized what a harpy she was.

"Zoe, honey," Brian called, "let's go to the party." He kept his voice happy, even though he wanted to wring Barbara's neck.

"Am I still going to Kimmy's, or do I have to go with Mommy?"

"You're going to Kimmy's tomorrow, and next weekend you're with Mommy." Brian walked over to where she stood on the third step, and she jumped into his arms. "Now let's go see Uncle Dieter and Uncle Gerald." Brian laughed as he whisked her off her feet and out the door, Barbara's drama soon forgotten as they climbed into the car.

The drive from the northern Milwaukee suburbs to the East Side, where Dieter and Gerald lived, took awhile. As they rode, Zoe watched for Christmas lights, her face nearly plastered to the glass of the backseat window. "Look," she said, pointing just down the street as they pulled up to Gerald and Dieter's house.

"That's their neighbors. They will be at the party, and I bet you could get Uncle Dieter to take you over there if you ask nicely." Brian turned off the engine, and he heard Zoe unfasten her seat belt. Brian got out and opened her door, letting her walk in front of him as they navigated their way to the front door and rang the bell.

"Uncle Dieter," Zoe cried as the door swung open, and she rushed forward to get a hug. Gerald was right behind and he got a hug as well before their coats were taken upstairs. "Where's the candy tree?" she asked excitedly, and Dieter took her hand and led her into the living room where Brian heard a gasp. "There's lollipops too!"

"Yes, and you can have a candy cane now, and when you go home, I promise you can have some lollipops. I have a special bag all set aside for you."

Brian joined them in the living room in time to see Zoe take a candy cane off the enormously tall tree that seemed to have more lights on it than Brian thought humanly possible.

"Brian, would you like a drink?" Gerald asked from behind him.

"Please," Brian answered as he followed him into the kitchen. "So, did you enjoy your day off yesterday?" Brian asked after Gerald handed him a glass of red wine.

"Yes. But we spent most of the day getting ready for the party," Gerald answered with a grin. Technically, Brian was Gerald's managing partner at the law firm, but over the past year, since he'd had the courage to tell Gerald he was gay, Gerald and his partner Dieter had become very good friends with Brian.

"So, Brian," Dieter said from behind him, "have you heard anything about the appeal?"

"Yes, just yesterday, as a matter of fact. The hearing is scheduled for early February." Dieter's great-grandfather and his daughter had escaped from Austria just ahead of the Nazis. His great-grandfather had had a sizable art collection, including four landscapes as well as a portrait of his wife, Anna, painted by August Pirktl, a well-known Austrian painter. Those five paintings were the subject of a lawsuit against the Austrians that Gerald won for Dieter. The decision was now being appealed, as they had known it would be, and both Gerald and Dieter had asked Brian to handle the appeal. Gerald felt he was too close to the situation to handle it properly. Brian had been honored, and with Gerald's initial success had come a string of art-recovery cases that had kept Gerald and Brian busy enough that they had both become top producers at the firm. There was even talk of making Gerald a partner already.

"That's really good." Dieter was pleased but cautious. They'd already spent a year waiting for the appeal hearing. "I'm trying not to get too excited because I know even if we win, it'll be appealed again."

"It's all a step in the process."

"I know," Dieter answered, and Brian wished all his clients could be as understanding and patient as Dieter. "Gerald and I are planning a trip back to Vienna this summer, and we wanted to ask if you and Zoe here would like to go along." The doorbell rang, and Dieter excused himself, taking Zoe with him.

"Dieter has been corresponding with the family that owns the house his great-grandparents lived in. It's now a small hotel, and we're planning to stay there. They said in one of their letters that they found some things in the attic that might belong to his family, so he's really excited," Gerald explained. "And we thought if you wanted to go, we could see the city, take Zoe to a real palace, and you could see *The Woman in Blue* as well as the four landscapes that we've been fighting to get returned."

"I'd like that," Brian said before sipping from the glass. He hadn't had a real vacation in years, and it would be good to take Zoe away.

Dieter returned with Zoe and another man. "Brian, this is Reed. He and I work together." Dieter looked pleased with himself, and Reed smiled at him, extending his hand, and Brian shook it. "Why don't you two go on into the living room while Zoe and I finish putting out the food," Dieter said, scooting them out of the kitchen, and Brian knew he was truly being set up.

Following Reed, he walked into the living room. "Dieter has tried to set me up with you for the last three months," Reed said with a laugh. "He's so sweet." Reed sipped from his glass. "He tells me you're a lawyer."

"Yes. I work with Gerald." He left out the part about being his boss; that really wasn't important. "He and I now handle cases that involve the return of stolen and looted art. It keeps us very busy." Brian indicated the paintings on the walls. "These are some of the works we've recovered. So what do you do?"

"I'm a computer programmer," Reed answered as he looked around the room. It was fairly obvious to Brian that Reed wasn't particularly interested. Not that Brian had much experience, but there didn't seem to be much of a connection. The doorbell rang, and since no one was nearby, Brian answered it, and Mark and Tyler from up the street walked inside. Brian had been to parties at Gerald and Dieter's a few times, so he knew some of their friends. Brian said hello, and the doorbell rang again. More people arrived, and Dieter walked into the hall to greet them, and soon the house was filled with people. Brian had lost track of Reed, which seemed okay, since after awhile, he saw him speaking to another of Dieter and Gerald's friends, and the two men seemed quite cozy.

"Hi, Daddy," Zoe said from beside him.

"Are you having fun?" he asked his daughter, whose eyes seemed wide and her smile huge.

"Yes. They have great computer games, but I didn't want you to be lonely."

Brian lifted Zoe into his arms. "Thank you, honey. Did you want to show me the food you helped Uncle Dieter put out?" Brian put her down, and she led him into the dining room.

"Are you enjoying the party?" a voice said from behind Brian as he reached to get a plate. Brian turned and saw Reed smiling at him.

"Yes, very much," Brian answered. "You?" From the smile on the man's face standing next to him, Reed was definitely having a good time, or would be soon.

"Yes. Dieter and I have worked together for a few years, but this is the first time I've been able to attend one of his parties," Reed answered getting a plate and handing it to his companion before taking one for himself. "This is Jonathon," Reed said, introducing him before turning to his companion, "and this is Brian. He works with Gerald." The two of them shook hands, and Jonathon smiled a little and said hello before following Reed around the table as he filled his plate. It looked like Jonathon was staying close in case Reed tried to get away.

Brian felt a twinge of disappointment for a few seconds as he watched them. Granted, Dieter had tried to fix up him and Reed, but Brian wasn't really sure he was ready for anything, relationship or otherwise. He had Zoe, and she needed to come first. The divorce had been hard on her, especially with the way Barbara had gone off like she was free and really didn't seem to take much interest in her own daughter except when it suited her. Brian knew Zoe had been hurt, and he'd done his best to try to make up for it.

"Daddy." He heard Zoe's voice cut through his thoughts, and he bent down so he could hear her over the other conversations. "What's that man doing?"

Brian followed her gaze, looking toward the corner of the room, and saw two men standing together, motioning to each other with their hands. "They're using sign language," Brian explained without looking away. Their hand motions were so fluid, and the way they looked at each other made their connection seem so deep. Brian sighed softly, wishing he had that connection with someone else. Lord knew he'd never had it with Barbara. Not that he was surprised about that.

"Daddy," Zoe said impatiently, and he looked away from the two men.

"Sorry, honey." He turned to her and saw her huge blue eyes looking up at him. "They're talking with one another using their hands."

"But why?"

"Because at least one of them is deaf and can't hear," Brian explained to her, and she continued watching them, her plate dipping forward as her attention on it waned. Brian took the plate from her hand. "You shouldn't stare, honey. It's not nice. Let's get something to eat and find a place to sit down." Brian helped her with her food and placed two napkins in his pocket before finding a quiet place to sit.

In one corner of the living room, Brian found two chairs and helped Zoe get settled on the floor. She folded her legs beneath her pink dress, using the seat of the chair as a table once Brian had put down a napkin first. Zoe ate quietly, and Brian looked around the room, seeing Harold, the senior partner at the law firm, and his wife, Christine, talking with another couple.

"Is there anything I can get for you?" Dieter asked as he passed through the room.

"No, thank you, we're good," Brian answered with a smile after swallowing his bite of hummus. "Everything is delicious. Did you make it all yourself?" Brian knew that Dieter was a good cook, and Brian was a bit jealous because he burned water on a regular basis.

"Yes," Dieter said with a pleased smile, looking at the fireplace. "Gram would roll over in her grave if I served store-bought food at a party." Dieter chuckled, and Brian did as well, having heard the stories of the old-fashioned grandmother who had raised Dieter from the time his parents had died when he was four. "I'm glad you like it."

"Daddy, I'm full," Zoe pronounced before handing Brian her plate.

"You can take a lollipop off the tree," Dieter told her, and Brian saw Zoe's eyes go wide. "And I believe there's a present under the tree for you."

Brian watched as Dieter took Zoe to the tree. She chose one of the brightly colored lollipops, and then Dieter handed her a wrapped present. Brian saw her sit on the floor before tearing open the present, letting loose a squeal of delight that cut though every conversation in the house. "I love it. Thank you," she said before hugging Dieter. Then Brian saw Zoe tear by him, carrying what looked like a DVD in her hand, and Brian followed her with his eyes. He heard Gerald's voice and another, "Thank you, I love it." Deciding his daughter was in good hands, Brian sat back and relaxed, talking to the people around him like an adult.

Over the past year, his main companion outside of work had been Zoe, and Brian hadn't realized how much he missed adult company and conversation until he was deep in a conversation with Harold about his upcoming deep-sea fishing trip to Florida. God, it had been a long time since he'd simply talked to another adult.

"I'm sorry to interrupt," Dieter said, and Brian and Harold paused their conversation. "I'm taking Zoe up to the television room so she can watch her video."

"Thank you," Brian said, grateful to his friend. Dieter left, and Brian and Harold continued their conversation. After a while, Harold excused himself and got up. Brian, deciding he wanted another glass of wine, walked through the house to the kitchen. The room was full of people, and Brian poured a glass of wine and was about to leave when he lightly bumped into another man. Pausing to excuse himself, Brian stopped and the tall man turned around. Bright blue eyes stared into Brian's, and for one of the few times in his life, Brian stared open-mouthed, completely at a loss for words. This man was *stunning,* rather than beautiful, with piercing eyes that nearly made him flinch and deep black hair that shone in the light against his olive-toned skin. "I'm sorry," Brian said, for bumping him, and the man smiled slightly, nodding his head before turning away.

People shifted in the kitchen as glasses were filled and new faces moved to the bar for refills. Brian made his way back into the living room and nearly bumped into Gerald, thankfully not spilling any of his wine. "Who's the man over there with the dark hair?" Brian indicated the man he'd seen in the kitchen.

Gerald smiled at him. "That's Nicolai Romanov. He's an art restorer, and he's been helping Dieter with the paintings. He's a really sweet man," Gerald said, lowering his voice, "and very handsome. He's also available, or so I understand."

"What about the man with him?" Brian asked, his eyes following Nicolai and the other man around the room. They looked rather cozy to him.

"That's Peter, and they're not a couple. He's a friend and sort of acts as Nicolai's interpreter because he's deaf. Besides, Peter's as straight as an arrow, and if there were a lot of women here, Nicolai wouldn't be getting as much interpreting time. Peter's a bit of a ladies' man. Come on, I'll introduce you. Nicolai reads lips, so speak clearly and look at him, and you'll be fine." Before Brian could stop him, Gerald was leading him into the hallway where Nicolai was looking closely at one of the paintings. Gerald lightly touched him on the shoulder and stepped back.

"Nicolai," Gerald said once he'd turned around, "this is Brian." He noticed that Gerald made eye contact and spoke clearly, but not loudly, to Nicolai, who held out his hand.

"Very pleased to meet you," Nicolai said slowly, his consonants very smooth, and it took some concentration, but Brian was able to understand him. Brian shook his hand and wondered what to say. Thankfully Gerald started things off.

"I work with Brian. He and I try to get art works returned to their proper owners. Brian is handling *The Woman in Blue* case for Dieter and me," Gerald explained, and Brian saw Nicolai's eyes light up.

"That must be exciting," Nicolai said. "Dieter has told me about his great-grandmother. It is a very exciting story." Brian saw Nicolai's fingers and hands moving, presumably out of habit.

"Daddy." Zoe barreled into him laughing before turning to her Uncle Dieter. "I turned off the player."

"Zoe," Brian said, still looking at Nicolai, "this is Mr. Romanov."

"Hello." She suddenly seemed shy, and Brian hugged her to his side.

"Nicolai, this is my daughter Zoe." Brian made sure to face Nicolai so he could read his lips.

"Hello, Zoe," Nicolai said as he signed, and Brian heard Zoe inhale in surprise as she watched Nicolai's hands. "Zoe," Nicolai said rather clearly as he slowly signed her name. Zoe brought up her hands and began to move them, mimicking the movements. Nicolai gently corrected her fingers, and soon Zoe could sign her name. "Nic," Nicolai said and then performed the signs for his name. Brian found himself watching every movement of Nic's graceful hands, trying to make the signs himself along with his daughter.

"Like this," Nicolai told him, and Brian nearly jumped when the handsome man touched his fingers, lightly caressing his skin as he coached him through the signs. Brian repeated the movements for the three letters, and Nicolai smiled his encouragement. Brian wanted to ask Nicolai to teach him more signs, if only to get the other man to touch his hands again.

"Zoe," Tyler, who lived up the street, called as he approached. "A little bird tells me that you want to see the lights at our house."

Zoe turned to him, her eyes lighting up. "Can I, Daddy?"

"Sure, just get your coat from upstairs and be careful. It's slippery outside," Brian cautioned, regardless of the fact that it was falling on deaf ears. Zoe was already halfway up the stairs before he'd finished speaking. Tyler headed upstairs as well, and Brian concentrated his attention on Nicolai. "Do you only restore paintings?"

Nicolai shook his head before saying, "Glass windows too." Brian initially had trouble understanding, but the words made sense just as Nicolai pointed to the stained-glass window in the stairwell.

"Do you work for the art museum?"

"Yes," Nicolai answered. "I worked on their Monet." The look on his face told Brian that Nicolai was very proud of that, as he should be. Brian could only imagine being a restorer and being good enough to work on an important and valuable work like that.

"Gerald and I often have clients who need to have their art restored or repaired after we get it back. Would it be okay if I had them contact you?" As soon as the words were out of his mouth, he realized what a dumb question that was. He was at Gerald's party, and Gerald certainly knew how to get in touch with Nicolai. But he simply smiled and fished into his pockets before handing Brian a card.

"Best way is instant message or e-mail. If I am home, it is always on, except when I am working," Nicolai said.

"Would you like some wine?"

"Please," Nicolai said, and Brian nodded before making his way to the kitchen. Grabbing a bottle of water for himself, he wished he'd asked what kind Nicolai wanted, but guessed at a red and walked back into the hallway. Nicolai and another man, who Brian assumed was Peter, appeared to be having a conversation. Actually, they looked as though they were having a silent argument, with both of them signing frantically back and forth. Brian walked to Nicolai to offer him the glass, but he realized that it would limit Nicolai's ability to communicate, and it appeared from the near-manic signing that Nicolai would not appreciate that right now.

"Why did you drive me, then?" Nicolai asked and signed, his words very slurred and barely understandable.

"I didn't know I would meet someone," Peter said softly as he signed.

"Can I help?" Brian asked, and Peter turned to him, followed by Nicolai. "Zoe and I can give Nicolai a ride home if he needs one."

"Thank you," Nicolai said before turning to glare at his friend, signing something Brian figured was most likely obscene because Peter rolled his eyes and said good-bye before hurrying upstairs. "That was very nice."

Brian smiled and nodded before handing Nicolai the glass of wine. Peter came back down the stairs, carrying his coat and another one that obviously belonged to a woman. A bleached-blonde woman, apparently the only single woman at the party, walked over to Peter, and he helped her into her coat before the two of them waved good night and left. Nicolai raised his glass and made a rude gesture to his friend after the door had closed.

It opened again almost immediately, and Zoe rushed inside, her lavender coat fluttering as she moved. "Tyler showed me the lights and let me pet their dog. Her name's Jolie, and she likes to have her belly scratched." Zoe unzipped her coat and handed it to Brian.

"Why are you handing this to me? Do I look like a coat closet? Besides, we'll be going home in a little while. So you need to gather your things together and say good-bye and thank you to everyone," Brian told her as he handed back the coat, which Zoe immediately set in a corner before hurrying toward the kitchen. She returned shortly with Dieter and Gerald, and after saying good night and getting all of their coats, along with Zoe's gift and a bag with enough candy to send her into a sugar coma, they said their last good-nights and left the house.

Brian led them to the car, chirping it unlocked before making sure Zoe was buckled in as well as letting Nicolai get into the passenger seat. After walking around to the driver's side, Brian started the car and pulled away from the curb. "I live in Whitefish Bay," Nicolai explained rather clearly, and Brian drove through the city streets, heading toward the near northern suburbs. Nicolai's home was right on the way, and it didn't take long for them to reach his home. "Thank you for the ride," Nicolai said before opening his door and getting out of the car.

"You're welcome," Brian said, making sure Nicolai could see him. Then the door closed, and Brian pulled away and down the street. As he approached the corner, he thought he could still see Nicolai standing on the sidewalk watching them, but he wasn't sure, and after he'd stopped, the figure he'd seen was gone.

Brian drove the rest of the way home, Zoe already dozing by the time they pulled into the driveway. Brian carried her inside, setting her on the sofa. "Go upstairs and get ready for bed. I'll be up soon." Without saying anything, Zoe began climbing the stairs, and Brian returned to the car, carrying in everything and putting it away before locking up the house and climbing the stairs. Zoe was already in her nightgown and in the bathroom brushing her teeth. When she was done, Brian joined her in her room, holding up the covers so she could climb into bed. "Good night, sweetheart," Brian said, kissing her on the forehead.

"Daddy, are you going to get married again?" Sometimes he wondered at the questions she came up with at the weirdest times. "'Cause if you do, will I have an evil stepmother like Cinderella?"

"Go to sleep, honey. I don't plan to get married, and I would never give you an evil stepmother. I promise." He kissed her once more before turning off the light and leaving the room. He quietly descended the stairs and picked things up as he made a sweep of the house before ending up in the family room in front of the television. God, he was tired, but not quite sleepy. The phone rang and he grabbed for it. "Hello."

"Brian, what's with this check?"

Barbara, just what he needed at this hour!

"What check are you talking about? Are you drunk?"

"No," she replied quickly and too indignantly, leading Brian to believe he was spot-on with his assessment. "I'm talking about my alimony check. It's too small. Where's the rest of the money?"

"Did you even bother to read our agreement? It states that after a year, the amount is reduced by a quarter for six months, and then another quarter for six months." It had felt really good to write the lower amount on the check. "You need to get a job and make sure you can support yourself, because in five months, the amount goes down again and then stops after six months, and you're on your own." *God help us all.*

"I didn't understand what all that meant," she sputtered, and Brian knew she'd at least had too much to drink.

"Ignorance will get you nowhere, and I'm not sending you a dime more, so you'd better start looking for a job so you can support yourself. You have a degree—you need to put it to use." He so did not need this now. Brian was tired and worn out. "I put you in touch with a career counselor. He should have been able to help you." Brian sighed from sheer tiredness. "I know you think I'm being mean to you, but you need to get on with your life, and getting a job will help you. You'll be in charge of your own money and your own destiny instead of dependent on someone else," Brian said, figuring he'd try reasoning with her. "Look, it's late and I'm really tired. Think about it, okay?"

"I don't care. I'm not getting off this phone until you send me more money," she harped, and Brian seriously wondered what had happened to the woman he'd married. Sure, they hadn't been in love, but they'd been civil, and Brian had cared for her, but those feelings were just memories as he listened to what she'd become.

"Good night, Barbara." She continued talking and Brian quietly hung up the phone, turning off the ringer so it wouldn't wake Zoe. Turning on the television, he curled under a blanket, watching whatever was on, or at least pretending to watch television.

Nicolai. Brian had never felt such an attraction to anyone in his life, and when Nicolai had touched his hands, Brian had had to stop himself from moaning out loud. He'd touched Barbara and been touched by her. She was the only person who'd ever laid a hand on him in an intimate way, but with one touch from Nicolai, Brian realized everything that he'd been missing for the past nine or so years. Not that he'd have given up having Zoe for anything, but with a simple touch Nicolai had shown him, whether he meant to or not, that there was something more than what he'd experienced.

Yawning widely, Brian turned off the television and quietly went upstairs, peering in on Zoe, asleep like an angel, before undressing, cleaning up, and climbing into his own bed.

*C*HAPTER 2

NICOLAI walked to his closet, trying to decide what to wear to dinner. Dieter had texted him earlier in the week, inviting him to the house on Friday night. He wished he'd asked if it was just him or if there were other guests. He sort of hoped that Brian would be there, but that was wishful thinking. They'd only conversed, such as it was, for a short time, but Nicolai had liked the way Brian had talked so Nicolai could see what he was saying, even when he was talking to his daughter. That had been sweet and something people he'd just met rarely did. It made it so much easier for him to follow a conversation when he saw both sides of it. Reading lips was not often exact, and the more clues Nicolai had as to what was being said, the more he understood. He'd gotten used to it.

Dieter had said to dress casually, even jeans, so Nicolai had pulled on his most fashionable pair and was trying to decide on a shirt. He wanted something nice, but didn't want to look stuffy. Settling on a long-sleeved polo, he pulled off the sweatshirt he'd been wearing and pulled the polo over his head before checking himself in the mirror. *Yes, this looks right.* He finished getting dressed and then hurried to the kitchen to get a bottle of wine before grabbing his coat. Before leaving, he did one more check of the house to make sure everything was okay. For most people, things had alarms and made sounds when something happened. Around Nicolai's house, it was all visually cued, but that meant he had to look for things. Seeing that everything was okay, Nicolai left the house, locking it before getting in his car. Thankfully, this time he wasn't relying on Peter for a ride home.

The drive didn't take long, and Nicolai parked before walking up to the house and pressing the doorbell. He remembered once standing on some friends' front step for five minutes, ringing their bell, only to find out it wasn't working. So now if no one answered, he always knocked too. Thankfully, the door swung open, and Dieter ushered him inside with a smile and a hug, which he returned before handing him the wine, seeing Dieter say, "Thank you."

Sometimes Nicolai wished he could actually hear what people were saying, and there were times when he wondered how the rest of the world could think with all that sound going on to distract them. Dieter pointed toward the living room, and Nicolai nodded, walking into the room. The first thing he saw was the tree blazing in the corner with what looked like a million lights. The second thing was Brian standing in front of the sofa, smiling at him. "Hello," he saw Brian say as he held out his hand. Nicolai took it and felt the same excited feeling he'd felt before, when he'd touched Brian to help him make the signs. "How are you?"

"I am fine and you?" Nicolai answered and saw by his expression that Brian understood him.

"Very good." Brian sat back down, and Nicolai did the same before turning around to look when he felt the floor vibrate slightly as Dieter came into the room with a small tray of glasses. He passed them out, and Gerald joined them as well, taking a glass and raising it in a silent toast before taking a sip.

"Dinner will be ready in a few minutes," Gerald said, facing him, and Nicolai smiled. Then to his surprise, both Gerald and Dieter left the room, so Nicolai looked to Brian for some idea of what was going on.

"You do realize that this is a fix-up," Brian said, and Nicolai widened his eyes. The thought had never occurred to him, and he wasn't sure how he felt about that. "Normally I would be offended, but tonight I don't mind," Nicolai saw Brian say, and he realized he didn't mind either. Rather than try to express his feelings verbally, Nicolai stood up and moved to sit next to Brian on the sofa.

"Have you always been deaf?" Brian asked. "Because you speak very well, and I understand that is a very difficult skill for a deaf person."

Nicolai formed his words carefully. Since he could not hear his own speech, he had to feel his words and that took extra time. "I wasn't born deaf, but I could never hear very well. I wore these big hearing aids when I was a kid, and it helped for a while, but by the time I was ten, I could barely hear anything at all. I faked it for a while, or at least I tried. I haven't heard a sound in almost twenty years. After I lost my hearing, I maintained my speech by using a computer program that translated speech into visual lines. Then when I matched the lines, I knew I was saying the word right. It takes a long time, and I still work with the program to make sure I stay understandable. I barely remember being able to hear now, but sometimes I wonder what it would be like," Nicolai said, watching Brian's face for his reaction. He expected some kind of pity—that was the reaction he usually got. Nicolai knew what it looked like. Their eyes would get all soft, and they'd look away. Their mouths would form this "O" shape, as if to say "Oh, I'm so sorry." Nicolai hated that shape and that look. But to his surprise, Brian showed none of that. His eyes looked at him levelly, meeting his gaze.

"I guess that's also why you're good at reading lips, because you could hear at one point," he saw Brian say, and Nicolai nodded slowly, not taking his eyes off Brian's. Mouths and lips were something Nicolai was very used to looking at, and his eyes traveled there almost of their own accord. He'd become adept at translating what people were saying, and he was used to the way people formed words. Of course, he could read some people better than others, and Brian seemed to speak clearly and levelly, making it easy for Nicolai to decipher what he was saying. However, Brian's lips fascinated him for another reason. They were full and sort of plump and really red. Raising his eyes from Brian's lips, he saw eyes looking back at him, almost into him, big, soft brown eyes that Nicolai could get lost in. He read faces all the time, and this was a face that he wanted to know more about.

Without thinking, Nicolai reached out to touch Brian's cheek and felt him jump. Pulling his hand away, Nicolai realized the liberty he'd taken and put his hand back at his side. He expected to see a rebuke in Brian's eyes, but his gaze moved to the doorway, and Nicolai followed it and saw Dieter standing there, smiling at both of them and gesturing toward the dining room. Nicolai was about to stand up when he saw Brian look back at him and smile before touching Nicolai's hand and then lifting it to his cheek. Now it was Nicolai's turn to smile.

Brian stood up, still holding his hand, before letting it go and motioning for Nicolai to go in front of him. "Thank you," Nicolai said before walking into the dining room and taking the seat Dieter indicated. Social situations like this were very hard for him because Nicolai knew that the conversation would go on around him and he would largely be left out. The food was passed and the scents drifted into his nose, making his stomach jump in anticipation—beef, carrots, mashed potatoes, not a fancy meal, but everything smelled and looked good. Nicolai filled his plate as the food was passed and then began to eat.

He'd taken two bites when he felt a light touch on his hand. Looking up, he saw Brian smiling at him, and Nicolai looked around the table for some clue as to what he'd missed, but he had no idea. That was why situations like this made him nervous. There was no way he could keep up with everything going on around him, and he knew it, so the easiest thing to do was withdraw. "I was wondering if you had any brothers or sisters," Nicolai saw Brian ask, and Nicolai set down his fork.

"I have a sister, Catherine. She's older than me by a few years," Nicolai answered carefully, seeing other people talking. He picked up some of what they were saying about their own brothers and sisters, but then returned to eating. It wasn't as though he didn't care or wasn't really interested, it was just that he'd watched enough "tennis games" at the dinner tables of friends to know he'd spend the next half hour bobbing his head back and forth just trying to keep up with the conversation. It was easier when someone signed— then he could pick up so much more, but that wasn't always possible, like today. Taking a few more bites, he tried to pay more attention and realized that Dieter was talking about how they'd met him.

"I've known Peter Barrett for a while, and he recommended me to help Dieter and Gerald review and clean their paintings. That was a few months ago, and we've since become friends," Nicolai explained, hoping he wasn't restating what had already been said. Nicolai saw everyone nod, and he went back to eating. He had no doubt that the conversation went on—he caught snippets of it, but he couldn't follow, so he ate and complimented Dieter on his cooking.

Brian once again touched his hand gently. "Dieter said that we will have dessert in a little while. He suggested that we would be more comfortable in the living room," Brian mouthed, and Nicolai nodded. He was much better one on one, and there were so many things he wanted to ask Brian. Pushing back the chair, he thanked both Dieter and Gerald for the wonderful food before walking toward the living room with Brian behind him.

Nicolai stopped along the way to look at one of Dieter's paintings. "I just finished cleaning this one," Nicolai said before turning around. "The colors are much more vibrant now. Do you know much about art?" Nicolai asked Brian, watching his lips carefully as he waited for an answer.

"I've learned a lot in the last few years, but it's mostly been from the legal or value perspective. Working on legal cases that involve art doesn't bring me into contact with the creative side of art," Brian mouthed, and Nicolai saw him move a little closer. For a second he thought Brian might be trying to kiss him, but he stepped back again, and Nicolai looked around, wondering if someone might have walked into the room, but it was only them. "Gerald and I have helped return many paintings, sculptures, and even a Tiffany window to their rightful owners, but I rarely ever actually get to see the pieces, and the only thing I know about most art is that you hang it on the wall."

Nicolai saw that Brian's lips were moving faster, and he'd had a difficult time deciphering everything he said, but he got most of it. Brian was nervous, or at least appeared to be, and Nicolai wondered why. If he was nervous because Brian liked him, then that was cute, but if he was nervous being around Nicolai because he was deaf and running out of things to say, then....

"I could show you around the museum, if you like. They have a nice collection," Nicolai offered carefully, watching Brian's eyes, and what he saw made him smile. Brian liked him, or seemed to like him. God, he felt as though he was a teenager again. "Would you like to go on Sunday? The museum is open in the afternoon." Nicolai suddenly felt some of the nerves he'd seen in Brian. "We could bring Zoe, if you like," Nicolai offered.

"Zoe's with her mother this weekend," he saw Brian say before motioning toward the living room. Nicolai sat on the sofa and Brian took the seat next to him, turning so they could see one another. "I married Barbara just after college," Brian said, and Nicolai found himself both reading and watching Brian's enthralling lips. "I didn't want to accept that I was gay, and I slept with Barbara and she got pregnant, so I married her. It took me years to figure out that what she really wanted was to be Mrs.—" Nicolai didn't understand and motioned for Brian to repeat himself. "Mrs. Lawyer," he said, and Nicolai nodded. "I was faithful to her the entire time we were married, and then I caught her cheating, so I filed for divorce."

"How old is Zoe?" Nicolai asked.

"She's nine, and just amazing." The smile on Brian's face as he talked about his daughter warmed the room. "I have custody of her, and Barbara gets her every other weekend—that is, when she bothers to actually follow through."

"How long have you been divorced?" Nicolai asked, wanting to know as much about Brian as he could. He seemed like such a sweet man, and Nicolai wondered why Barbara would have let him get away from her.

"Less than a year."

"Have you been with anyone?" Nicolai asked, and then he wished he hadn't. "I'm sorry. That's too personal."

"No. I haven't," Brian answered. "I have Zoe, and I know I need to be careful. She doesn't know about me, no one does except Gerald and a few other people. My sister does, though. Does your family know you're gay?"

"Yes. I told them years ago. They accepted it for the most part," Nicolai said. "I was in a relationship for about five years, but we broke up about a year ago, I guess." Nicolai felt Brian take his hand.

"I know how that feels. Even though Barbara and I were never really in love, ending the relationship was still hard. I'll understand if it's hard to talk about, but I'll listen if you want to talk."

Nicolai shrugged. "It's not hard anymore, but it was. I thought Justin was the one for me, but about a year ago he told me he wanted to move on. He said there wasn't someone else, just that he didn't love me anymore. I think it got too hard."

"What?" Brian asked, his face full of concern.

"It can be hard living with someone with sensory challenges, and I know he always thought he had to help me and be there for me. I think it was my fault because I relied on him too much and used him to help me too much. It's hard to explain, but I sometimes think I used his hearing to replace what I didn't have. Since he left, I've relearned how to do things I always could, but didn't have to when Justin was around."

"I read once that blind people sometimes lose some of their ability to find their way around when they rely on a sighted companion. Is it like that?"

"Yes. I think that's it exactly. I wasn't reading lips very well, and my speech had become very sloppy because Justin did most of my talking for me." Nicolai saw Brian look away, and then Dieter walked into the room, setting a tray on the coffee table with what looked like an incredible chocolate dessert. Dieter cut a piece and handed it to him before pointing to the whipped cream. "Yes, thank you," Nicolai responded.

Dieter placed a dollop onto his plate before dishing out portions to the others. Nicolai sat back and slowly ate his dessert. For the last little while, he and Brian had talked, really talked. Nicolai hadn't realized how long it had been since he'd connected with someone like that. It seemed funny, but even though they talked about his deafness, Nicolai hadn't felt deaf when he'd been with Brian. But as soon as everyone else joined them, the wall went back up between him and everyone else. He couldn't follow all the conversations because he wasn't sure whose lips to look at. Eventually, he settled on Brian's and tried to follow along, and it worked, but only to a degree. He caught most of what was being said and even managed to add to the conversation, but he knew he was missing things.

"The cake was delicious," Nicolai said as he placed his empty plate on the tray before sitting back and trying to concentrate on the conversation. Dieter seemed to be asking Brian about a lawsuit involving some paintings.

"As I said, the appellate hearing is in early February, and we'll be ready. The original hearing was solid, so the only argument they can realistically make is the national-sovereignty issue, and we're ready for that."

"Can I ask what lawsuit you're talking about?" Nicolai asked. He'd been working on Dieter's paintings, but no one had told him about a lawsuit.

Brian touched his arm lightly, and he looked to him. "Dieter's involved in a lawsuit to get back some of his family's paintings. Are you familiar with *The Woman in Blue*?" Brian asked.

"Yes." He turned to Dieter.

"She's my great-grandmother, and that painting should belong to my family, along with four other Pirktl landscapes. The lawsuit is to try to get them back."

"That's amazing. I have loved that painting since I was in college, and it's a portrait of your great-grandmother?" Nicolai asked, wanting to make sure he understood all he was being told, because this was almost too good to be true. "*The Woman in Blue,* one of the most important paintings of the early twentieth century, is a portrait of your great-grandmother and belongs to you?"

"It should belong to my family, yes," Nicolai saw Dieter say. "We won at trial, but the Austrians are appealing, because Gerald...." Dieter took Gerald's hand in his own, and Nicolai saw how much in love they were simply by the look on Dieter's face, and he felt his breath catch. Justin had never looked at him like that, not really. Nicolai pulled himself out of his thoughts as Dieter continued. "Gerald figured out that the Austrians made money on the paintings here in this country, so we sued them here. That seems to be what the appeal is about, but both Gerald and Brian are brilliant, so I know we're going to win."

Nicolai saw what Dieter said, but his face and the position of his body said something very different. Dieter was nervous and scared, despite his words. "I hope you do," Nicolai said, turning to Brian and seeing a touch of Dieter's doubt in his eyes as well. Then Brian stifled a yawn, and Nicolai checked his watch, realizing just how late it was. Nicolai got up, and the others did as well. Dieter retrieved his coat, and Nicolai said good night to everyone. When he got to Brian, he was surprised when, instead of a handshake, he got a hug good night.

Brian's arms felt so good around him. He hadn't been held by anyone since Justin, and toward the end that had slipped out of their relationship. To Nicolai's surprise, he even felt his body react, and while he hoped Brian didn't realize it, the sensation made him feel alive in a way he hadn't in a while.

Then Brian released him and stepped back. "Should I pick you up on Sunday for the museum about one?"

"That would be nice," Nicolai answered before saying good night one more time and leaving the house, walking to his car.

The drive home along streets lined with houses twinkling with Christmas lights didn't take long, and Nicolai parked around the back in his garage, walking through the yard to the back door. Unlocking the door, he walked inside and saw that there was a light on in the front of the house. Cautiously, he peered into the living room. "Justin? What are you doing here?"

Nicolai saw Justin get up and walk over to him. "I wanted to see how you were doing," Justin signed.

"I'm fine," Nicolai signed in return, wondering what Justin really wanted. "I was having dinner with friends," he added. "How did you get in the house? You gave me your key when you moved out."

Justin colored slightly. "I used the one you hide in the garage. You haven't returned any of my messages, and I wondered if you were okay." Justin's fingers made the signs easily and fluidly.

"That's because I didn't have anything to say to you. You left me, remember? And I've spent the last year getting over you and moving on with my life. Then I start getting messages from you and now you show up in my house. What is it you really want?" Nicolai's fingers flew as some of his frustration slipped into his movements. "And please don't insult both of us by saying you made a mistake and want me to take you back or some such crap."

"I wasn't," Justin signed and then looked away. "Well, maybe I was. I've missed you for months, and I have been a fool." If anyone had ever managed to sign pitifully, it was Justin at that moment, and to make matters worse, Nicolai felt himself falling for it. Justin moved closer, and Nicolai knew he should have stopped him, but he didn't. The light touch on his arm felt so familiar, so warm and comforting.

Nicolai closed his eyes and let himself remember what it had been like when he and Justin had first met, the rush of excitement, the way his heart raced when Justin so much as touched him. Justin's arms pulled him close, hands rubbing along his back, the familiar scent of his cologne filling Nicolai's nose. He hadn't thought he'd ever feel these arms again or smell that combination of aftershave, cologne, and something purely Justin again, but he was. And if Nicolai were truthful, he'd wished for this moment for months after Justin had moved out, and now it was here. But Nicolai didn't feel what he expected to feel. The touch held no spark, and the aftershave simply mixed with the smell of sweat. Justin kissed him, something Nicolai had dreamed about at night.

After Justin had left, Nicolai had dreamed of being held and kissed again. Their breakup had been so abrupt—one day Justin was sleeping next to him, and the next he was gone.

"Justin," Nicolai said as he broke the kiss and moved away from his former partner and lover, hoping he conveyed some form of annoyance. "What are you doing?" Nicolai signed.

"Like I said, I missed you and I was wrong to leave you like I did," Justin signed back, a rather pathetic look on his face.

"What is it you want?" Nicolai asked, his fingers forming the signs as he asked the question verbally. "You've been gone a year, and suddenly you show up again and act as though nothing has happened and we can just pick up where we left off. I cannot do that," Nicolai signed emphatically. "I think there's more to this than you wanting me back, because if you did, you'd have come back

sooner. You're here for something, and I want to know what it is."
Nicolai finished signing his message before glaring at Justin,
actually feeling rather proud of himself. "When you left, I felt lost
and cut off from my own life for weeks. I trusted you and relied on
you. I counted on you for so many everyday tasks, like talking to
clients, simple things that are difficult for me, like answering the
phone. Things I took for granted because I had you. It took me a
long time to get over that and move on with my life, but I have, and
I am not interested in going back. Not now, not ever," Nicolai said
as he signed. He knew his voice was loud because he could feel it in
his throat and see Justin's reaction. Nicolai rarely yelled with his
voice, but he was very good at yelling with his hands.

"I'm sorry I hurt you," Justin signed slowly, his face a mask of
contrition. "I love you."

"Don't," Nicolai signed as he glared at Justin. "I don't think
you know what love is. When things got a little tough and we had to
tighten our belts, instead of sticking it out and helping, you bailed on
me." The soft look on Justin's face was almost enough to make him
relent... almost.

"I know," Justin signed, "and I was wrong."

"We agree on something, then. What is it you want?" Nicolai
knew he was being harsh, but he'd been with Justin for five years,
and he knew when Justin was angling for something.

"I just want you," Justin signed, his expression an angelic look
that had always seemed to melt Nicolai's resistance. It seemed to be
working this time as well, because Nicolai could feel his anger and
resentment slipping away. Justin stepped closer, a hand touching his
arm, the heat from Justin's hand radiating through Nicolai's shirt.

A short buzzing in his pants pocket made Nicolai jump slightly
and he stepped back, reaching to retrieve his phone. Nicolai loved
the advent of text messaging, a communication medium perfectly
made for him. Nicolai didn't recognize the number, but he opened
the message.

This is Brian. Got your number from Dieter and
I wanted to thank U for a wonderful evening.
Am looking forward to seeing you on Sunday.
Was wondering if I could take you to lunch
before we go to the museum.

His phone buzzed again with another message:

Wanted you to know that I am asking you on a
date. Looking forward to seeing you.

Nicolai smiled as he read the second message. Looking up, he realized that Justin was peering over his shoulder. Nicolai turned so Justin couldn't see. "You're seeing someone else?" Justin signed, his face communicating hurt surprise.

"I met someone at a friend's party a few days ago, yes. His name is Brian." Nicolai stopped, realizing this was none of Justin's business, and he switched thoughts. "Why shouldn't I be seeing someone? You've been gone a year, and I'm allowed to find someone new. Look, I don't know what you want or why you picked now to show up again, but I think it's best if you leave." Nicolai walked to the front door and opened it. "Good night, Justin," he said.

Justin walked toward him, and Nicolai hoped he'd leave, but Justin stopped in front of him. "I do love you, Nicolai." Nicolai didn't know what to say, or quite what he felt. It had taken a lot of effort and heartache for him to get over Justin, and Nicolai didn't think he could trust him again, at least not with his heart.

"Good night," Nicolai answered. He knew he seemed heartless, but he knew Justin, and any sign of weakness would be seen as an opening for him to press his advance. "I'm sorry, Justin, but I don't love you, at least not like I did." Nicolai held out his hand. "My key," he added, and he waited until Justin fished it out of his pocket and placed the key in his hand. Nicolai closed his fingers around it as Justin left. Justin didn't say anything as far as Nicolai could tell, but he had little doubt that this wasn't the last he'd see of Justin. The man was tenacious when he wanted something. Closing the door, Nicolai leaned against it, his heart pounding in his chest. He felt as though he'd just passed some sort of test. Breathing deeply, he smiled as he realized he was truly over Justin. He wasn't interested in him anymore. He and Justin had had a number of good years together, and Nicolai would probably have spent the rest of his life with Justin if Justin hadn't left him. Fishing his phone out of his pocket, Nicolai answered the last of Brian's text messages.

I had a great time too. Looking forward to seeing you on Sunday. A lunch date with you sounds great. Please let me know where to meet.

Nicolai sent the message and then made sure the house was locked before setting the key Justin had given him in the bowl on the table in the entrance hall. He turned out the lights and headed upstairs to bed. After cleaning up and turning out the lights in the bedroom, Nicolai climbed into bed, getting comfortable before closing his eyes, letting the images that made up his thoughts settle, and soon he fell asleep.

NICOLAI stood in his living room, peering out the window as he waited for Brian to pick him up for their lunch date. When he saw the blue BMW pull up in front of the house, he got his coat and met Brian on the walk. Brian smiled at him, a big, happy smile, and Nicolai returned it. "Hello," Brian signed, and Nicolai smiled. It wasn't quite right, but the thought that Brian went to the effort to learn was gratifying. "I thought we could have lunch near the museum, if that is okay," Brian asked, obviously having reached the limit of his signing ability.

"I trust you," Nicolai said and signed before letting Brian lead him to the car. Conversation in the car was difficult because Nicolai couldn't see Brian's lips, so he sat and rode through town until Brian parked in front of a small restaurant in what had once been a house. Nicolai saw Brian turn off the car, and then he turned toward him. "I have never been here before, but it looked nice and I thought we could try it."

"It seems nice," Nicolai replied before following Brian inside. A lady spoke to Brian, and Brian touched his hand, motioning slightly for him to follow her. All the tables appeared full, and Nicolai saw people laughing and talking, but the room itself, like everything else, was totally silent to him. Sitting down in the chair, he took the menu the young woman offered and opened it, looking over the selections. When he lowered the menu, he saw another young woman looking at him expectantly, and Nicolai looked over at Brian, who motioned slightly toward his glass. Nicolai pointed to the beer he wanted, and the server smiled before leaving the table.

"You look very nice," Brian mouthed, and Nicolai smiled.

"So do you," he said softly, and Brian mouthed a thank-you. A glass was set down in front of him, and Nicolai looked up at the server. He could tell she was speaking, but she wasn't looking at him enough that he could read her lips. Nicolai saw Brian stop her, and then she turned toward him, her face red as she explained their sea-bass special. Nicolai indicated that he'd have that, and she asked him a lot of questions. She spoke fast, and Nicolai hoped he'd understood her properly. She seemed happy with his answers, but Nicolai had learned in the past that even when he thought he'd ordered correctly, sometimes he got things he wasn't expecting. "Did I order okay?" Nicolai asked.

Brian nodded. "Yes. You ordered just fine. By the way, I know you can't tell, but you have a great voice, really deep and rich-sounding. Sort of like the voice of God." Nicolai saw Brian lean slightly over the table, like he was about to share a secret. "It's sexy," he mouthed, and Nicolai nearly laughed. "What is so funny?"

"A deaf man with a sexy voice," Nicolai replied before putting his hand over his mouth to try to stifle his laughter. "I guess it's like a blind man being exceedingly attractive. It's sort of irrelevant for me, but I'm glad you like it."

Nicolai took a drink from his beer glass, setting it down as the server placed a salad plate in front of him. It appeared that he'd ordered the correct dressing, at least. Nicolai began to eat, watching Brian between bites, but thankfully he didn't try to carry on a conversation. Nicolai knew that most people talked when they ate, especially on a date, but under the best circumstances, that was hard for him since his primary method of communication, his hands, were otherwise engaged.

Brian set down his knife and fork, and Nicolai did the same. "I noticed that you don't try to converse much when you eat." Brian's face contained a definite hint of mirth. It had been a long time since he'd been with someone who could joke with him without being insulting.

"I've found out from personal experience that signing while holding a knife and fork is dangerous, not to mention exceedingly messy," Nicolai quipped, hoping he sounded like he was making a joke. Brian's smile told him he'd been successful. Humor was exceedingly difficult for him. It wasn't that he didn't have a sense of humor, but since he couldn't hear his own voice, he couldn't really make sure he sounded the way he wanted, so he usually remained serious—it was just safer.

After they'd finished their salads, the server brought their main courses, and Nicolai settled in to eat. The fish was delicious, and he said so to Brian, inquiring about his beef. As he was finishing, Nicolai felt a soft tap on his arm, and he turned to see a small girl standing near him. A woman rushed up behind her and began saying something rather frantically before guiding the girl away. Nicolai signed hello, and the little girl's face lit up. She wriggled away from her mother and hurried back. "What's your name?" Nicolai signed, as the woman, most likely the girl's mother, hurried back, stopping once she saw them signing.

"Emily," the little girl signed, her eyes big and happy.

"I'm Nic," he signed in return. "How old are you?"

"Five," she signed. "How old are you?"

"Old," Nicolai signed exaggeratedly, and the little girl giggled. "Are you her mother?" Nicolai signed to the woman.

"Yes," she signed back. "I'm sorry we're interrupting your lunch, but Emily saw you signing earlier and insisted on coming over." She placed her hands protectively on Emily's shoulders, and Nicolai saw grief in her eyes and wondered at the source, but knew better than to ask.

"I'm glad she did. Where does she go to school?" Nicolai spoke as clearly as he could.

"The whole family is learning to sign at the Milwaukee Academy for the Deaf after we found out that Emily's younger brother was born deaf." Nicolai could see the mother speaking as she signed, and he saw her hands falter slightly, like a visual stutter.

Nicolai nodded and turned back to Emily with a smile. "Thank you for stopping to talk to me. It was very sweet of you."

Emily smiled and signed "thank you" before her mother took her hand and guided her away. Nicolai watched as she turned back to him and waved as they left the restaurant. Their server returned and asked something of Brian before placing the check on the table. Nicolai reached for it and received a momentary scowl from Brian, so he pulled his hand away. After checking the bill, Brian handed it back to the server along with his credit card.

"You can get it next time," Brian told him, and Nicolai smiled before signing a thank-you. Brian's lunch treat was nice, but the idea of another date was even better. The server returned, and Brian signed the bill before standing up. After putting on their coats, they left the restaurant. "Would you like to walk?"

"Yes," Nicolai answered, and they crossed the street. "Thank you for lunch, that was very nice of you."

"You're welcome," Brian told him, turning his face so Nicolai could read his lips. "Emily was adorable."

"Yes, she was. At first I thought she was deaf, but I think she just knew how to sign."

"Emily could hear, I know that," Brian explained.

Nicolai swallowed, remembering the grief he'd seen in the mother's eyes. He decided to change the subject. "Is there something special you'd like me to show you when we're at the museum? You told me you had an appeal coming up for Dieter's case. I could show you the art of that period and try to explain some things about it."

Brian stopped. "That would be wonderful," Brian told him before continuing on. Once inside the museum, Brian paid the admission and then let Nicolai take the lead. "If I have questions, I'll ask, but I want you to just let me know what you want to tell me."

"What's the basis of your curiosity?" Nicolai asked, signing without giving it a second thought.

Brian motioned toward one of the benches, and Nicolai sat down, waiting for Brian to do the same. "I have the appeal for Dieter in less than two months, and there are a number of issues that the defendants are raising that I don't know anything about. *The Woman in Blue* is regarded as a national treasure, so they're pulling out all the stops. I can't defend against their arguments if I don't understand what they are."

"This appeal has you nervous?" Nicolai asked, already knowing the answer from the look in Brian's eyes.

"Yes. Gerald and Dieter are friends, good friends, and this means the world to Dieter. He is one of the sweetest people I have ever met, and I know it will break his heart if we lose."

"Okay. I think we'll start at the beginning and work forward. I'll do my best to give you a basic art education in a few hours." Nicolai patted Brian's leg before standing up and leading him through the museum.

They started at early religious art, and Nicolai picked a painting here or there to illustrate the basic concepts of art through time. "During Medieval times, all art was commissioned by the church. People couldn't read, so art was used to tell the church's stories. With the Renaissance, merchant classes developed, and art was commissioned by wealthy, private individuals," Nicolai explained as they walked from room to room. There was so much he could talk about, but he needed to keep it simple, so he stuck to the basics.

By the time they got to early twentieth-century art, Nicolai saw that Brian's eyes were beginning to glaze over. "This is the art of the time of *The Woman in Blue.* There was a lot happening at that time all over the Western world. Women got the right to vote, some of the old empires were crumbling, and society was changing rapidly. This led to a sense of freedom and exuberance that you can see in the art. Pirktl was famous and popular even while he was alive, and Anna must have been very wealthy and very beautiful to have convinced him to paint her portrait. He didn't do many," Nicolai explained, and from his expression Brian seemed to be hanging on every word. "This is a painting from that period. It's not nearly as important or as groundbreaking, but you can see some of the exuberance of the period." Nicolai looked at the tag near the painting. "This artist was definitely influenced by Pirktl."

"Why is *The Woman in Blue* so important?"

"Because it's loved. That's one of the hardest questions to answer in art. Why is one artist or a particular painting loved more than another? Some of it is hype and some is because the image touched people in a particular way. That the Austrians consider it a national treasure is irrelevant to the way it makes the viewer feel, and I suppose to your legal case, because it's a painting just like any of these. And it means something different to every person who sees it, but that should not have a bearing on whom the proper owner is." Before Nicolai knew what was happening, he felt himself being hugged tight. Nicolai wasn't sure what he'd done to deserve the hug, but it felt good, and he returned it.

Brian jerked and pulled away abruptly, and Nicolai wondered what had happened. Following Brian's gaze, Nicolai rolled his eyes as he saw Justin striding toward them with a thunderous look on his face. He was about to confront Nicolai when Brian stepped in the way, blocking him. Nicolai could not see what Brian was saying, but whatever it was took the wind out of Justin's sails very fast.

"Tell him I'm your boyfriend," Nicolai saw Justin sign.

"Brian," Nicolai began, feeling extremely embarrassed. "This is my *former* boyfriend Justin."

Brian turned to look at Nicolai. "The one who left you?"

Nicolai answered with a nod of his head, and Brian turned back around. Nicolai only got a glimpse of the look on Brian's face, but he knew he wouldn't want to be Justin about now. Brian stood his ground and even put his hands on his hips, glaring at the much bigger man as he walked away. "What did you tell him?" Nicolai asked once Justin was gone.

"That he needed to leave… now. It's hard to explain, but let's just say I used my lawyer voice."

Nicolai looked where Justin had gone. "I can take care of myself," Nicolai said. That was one of the issues he and Justin had had.

"I know. But with the way he was talking, I knew you couldn't hear him, so I stepped in to protect you. It was not an indication that I thought you couldn't take care of yourself—I didn't mean to insult you or anything," Nicolai saw Brian say before he reached into his pocket and pulled out his phone. Brian talked for a few minutes before hanging up. "Zoe will be home in an hour. Would you like to have dinner with us? I'll probably order a pizza, but I know Zoe would like to see you. She keeps asking about you."

"She does? Are you sure?"

"Yes, I'm sure. I like you, Nicolai, and I want Zoe to as well."

"But what if she gets to like me and things don't work out?" Nicolai asked, watching Brian's expression closely.

"Zoe's pretty smart. She'll figure things out before most people I know. She's also pretty resilient. She held up during the divorce better than I ever thought possible, and she does keep asking about you," Nicolai read on Brian's lips. "I promised myself when I decided I needed to live my life that I wasn't going to hide from my daughter. That doesn't mean I need to tell her everything, but if she asks, I will not lie to her, and I want her to meet the people in my life."

"Okay, if you're sure." Nicolai half smiled, still a little concerned. "I'd like to see your daughter again."

"Then if you're ready, we can walk back to the car," he saw Brian say and felt his hand on the small of his back, the touch gentle, but Nicolai felt the care in the touch.

They left the museum and walked over the bridge and along the street to where Brian had parked his car. He turned before opening the door. "I don't want to pressure you. I like you, Nicolai, and I don't want you to do anything you aren't comfortable with. I have to be home when Barbara drops off Zoe, but I can stop by your house on the way if that's what you want."

Nicolai knew that Brian was giving him a way out. "Then let's go. We don't want to be late for meeting your daughter." Nicolai saw Brian's smile as he opened the car doors. Nicolai got inside and buckled up before Brian pulled away from the curb. He watched the world pass outside the windows like he always did when he rode in a car, like he always watched everything as carefully as he could. When they parked in the driveway of Brian's house, Nicolai peered at the imposing house. He didn't know what he'd expected, but it hadn't been a place as big as this. Brian waited for him and then led him inside, motioning for him to have a seat in the family room while he turned on lights before sitting next to him.

Brian took his hand, holding it in his, skin warm against his. "There's something I've wanted to do all day." Brian brought his hand to his lips, placing a light kiss against the skin of his knuckles. Then a thumb lightly touched Nicolai's lips as Brian's eyes locked onto his. Brian moved closer, tilting his head slightly, and Nicolai's eyes closed and he waited until Brian kissed him. Their lips touched, lightly at first and then with slightly more force. Nicolai's breath caught as he kissed back. Then the simple, sweet touch ended as he saw Brian's daughter rush into the room, her lavender winter coat a blur as she raced into her father's arms. Nicolai saw Brian scoop her up before hugging her with a huge smile on his face, and Nicolai waited for them to say their hellos.

It wasn't very long before Zoe, her coat now a heap on the floor, held up her little hands and made the sign for hello and then N-I-C. He smiled and signed, "Hello, Zoe." She grinned and then raced away, her coat dragging behind. After a few minutes and without warning, she bounded onto the sofa, nearly scaring him half to death before sitting next to him. "Can you show me more?" Nicolai saw her ask, and he nodded.

"Please," Nicolai said and made the sign, placing his hand on his chest and making a circular motion to the left. Zoe did the same, smiling at him when he nodded. Nicolai saw her turn toward her dad and show him the sign. Brian hung up the phone—Nicolai hadn't realized he'd received a call—and joined their little sign-language lesson. They learned please, thank you, Daddy, hello, and good-bye, then Christmas and tree, the last two because of the twinkling Christmas tree in the corner. Eventually, Brian left them and returned with a huge pizza box, and Nicolai had to show them the signs for that, too, but not while they ate. Before it got too late, Brian got Zoe bundled up, and they took Nicolai home, each signing good-bye as he got out of the car.

CHAPTER 3

FOR Brian, Christmas and New Year's passed in a blur of torn paper, car rides to family and Barbara's, and Zoe's happy squeals as she got yet another present. Brian had cut back on his gifts to Zoe, concentrating on one larger gift rather than trying to get her everything on her list. The problem was that his mother simply bought everything Brian hadn't. It was a complete miracle that Zoe wasn't spoiled rotten.

"Hey, you look like you're a million miles away," Gerald said as he walked into his office, and Brian yawned and tried to cover it up, but failed. "Not sleeping?" Gerald sat down in one of the chairs across from his desk, placing the bag from the deli on Brian's desk.

"No. I keep thinking there's something I'm missing in this appeal for Dieter, and it's driving me crazy. Yet whenever I look over what I have, I can't find anything." Brian handed Gerald the paperwork on the case, but he simply took it without opening it.

"We've reviewed this case with every attorney in the office, and nobody can see that there's anything missing. But I'm going to give you the same advice you gave me when I tried this case—be alert and ready for anything. By the way, I can clear my schedule for the day of the hearing, so I can go with you as wingman if you'd like." Gerald had tried the original case, but had turned the appeal over to Brian because he was getting emotionally involved, and Brian could see a bit of that in himself now. They'd both become excited, and if Brian were honest, a bit nervous, as the appeal approached. This wasn't just any appeal. This was the chance for him and the firm to make a real name for themselves on a national level and set a potentially important precedent in this particular area of the law.

Gerald stood up and closed the door before returning to his chair, pulling his sandwich out of the bag. "Why the doubt? I have never seen you anything but supremely confident in court, even when you have a case everyone says in unwinnable. If this is about Dieter and me, then you should put that out of your mind. We both know that this is a bit of a long shot, but so was the original case, and we won there. Our argument for asking the courts to breach the national-sovereignty principle because they made money in the United States on the property in question is sound, and the other side is on the defense."

"Appeals are never that easy or straightforward. I saw a case when I was a student where the attorneys argued over the context of the word 'is' for a day and a half." Brian's sandwich sat on the flattened bag, unopened.

"I know, and that's why Dieter and I wanted you to handle it for us. You're the best, and I only get the best for him."

Brian leaned against his desk, sighing loudly. "Your partner is one of the kindest, sweetest people I have ever met, and I just don't want to be the one to disappoint him."

Gerald scoffed lightly before looking around. "Brian, you're my boss as well as my friend, so I'm going to tell you this as a friend. If we lose, Dieter will be disappointed, but in the justice system, not in you. So pull your head out of your butt and go for it." Gerald grinned and raised his eyebrows in that "you know I'm right" way he had, and Brian chuckled and began to open his lunch. "Now, speaking of kind, sweet people, what's going on with you and Nicolai?"

Brian felt himself smile. "We got together between the holidays, and we exchange text messages every day. He's been really busy restoring some new acquisitions for the museum, but we have a date this weekend." Brian didn't try to keep the excitement out of his voice. "We're taking things slowly, or at least I am. Communication is still difficult because I know he doesn't understand everything. Don't get me wrong, Nicolai is amazing, and Zoe loves him," Brian said before taking a bite of his sandwich.

Their conversation turned to their cases, and they talked legal strategy for the rest of their lunch. Packing their trash on the empty bag, Brian threw it away, and Gerald left his office. Brian went back to work, trying to concentrate, until he heard a soft knock on his door. Looking up, he saw Bernice, one of the admins, standing in the doorway. "I got a call from Jeanie in reception. There's a man in the lobby asking for you. He appears agitated, and Jeanie said he seems to be deaf, and she's having a difficult time communicating with him."

Brian jumped to his feet. "Is his name Nicolai Romanov?" Brian was already out of his office before she could answer. Striding toward the lobby, he opened the door and saw his Nicolai nervously pacing the floor. "It's okay, Jeanie, I have it from here," he told the receptionist when he saw her worried look. Stepping forward, Brian touched Nicolai on the shoulder. He jumped as he wheeled around, then a look of immense relief showed on his face. Brian motioned him inside and to his office, closing the door behind them. As soon as it clicked shut, Nicolai had his arms around Brian's waist, hugging him tight. Brian wondered what had happened, but he wasn't going to complain, whatever it was.

Catching Nicolai's eye, he gently asked, "What's wrong?"

Nicolai released the hug and reached for the bag he'd dropped onto the floor. Opening it, he fumbled for a second before withdrawing what looked like a letter and handing it to him. "Justin wants part of my house," Nicolai said, and Brian saw him signing like mad. "He says he paid for things while he lived there and is entitled to part of the house." Nicolai was barely understandable. Brian motioned for him to take a seat and read the letter.

"It's okay," Brian said before taking the chair next to Nicolai's. "This is just a letter from an attorney. People do this all the time to scare someone else into paying them. I know this attorney, and he'll do anything for a buck." The worried look on Nicolai's face tugged at Brian's heart. "Don't worry. I'll respond to this letter, and I'll scare the living daylights out of both Justin and the attorney."

"Thank you," Nicolai signed.

"You're welcome," Brian signed in return, hoping he'd done it right, and from Nicolai's smile, he guessed he had. "Why is Justin being so vindictive? What happened between the two of you?"

"We were good together for a long time, and then I wasn't getting a lot of work because the economy tanked and the museums had to cut back on some of their projects. I asked Justin to start helping with some of the expenses around the house, and he agreed. I thought things were okay, but a few weeks later, he said he was leaving. I wondered what I'd done for a long time, but now I think he was always about money and him having as easy a life as possible."

"Has he been contacting you?" Nicolai shook his head. "Okay. I'll draft a letter, and we can go over it before I send it. You have nothing to worry about. He has no claim on your house or anything else of yours. If he tries to press it, we'll prove that he lived with you for free for three years, and we'll ask for three years of back rent. That should stop him in his tracks." Brian saw Nicolai thank him again and changed tack. "There's something I've wanted to ask you. I have to go to Chicago for the appeal next month, and I was wondering if you would like to come along with me. I was going to get a hotel for the night before the hearing so I wouldn't be late, you know, held up in traffic or something."

Nicolai thought for a while, and Brian began to wonder if he'd understood him, then he said, "I have an appointment at the Art Institute for next month. I'll see if I can reschedule it for the same time as your court date. They're looking for someone to review the condition and stability of their Chagall windows. That's one job I would love to get. Can I let you know?"

"Of course," Brian said, looking at Nicolai. Brian always exaggerated his speech when he was talking to Nicolai, and it amazed him how much Nicolai seemed to understand. "I need to get back to work, but I'll text you tonight, and I'll see you in a few days. I have so much I can't wait to tell you." Brian stood up and opened his office door, walking Nicolai back toward the reception area. Brian signed good-bye, and Nicolai did the same, adding something to the end that Brian committed to memory so he could try to look it up.

"I didn't know you knew sign language," Jeanie said from behind her desk as she paused her typing.

"I'm just starting to learn," Brian said as he watched the elevator doors close.

"Jesus," she said lightly, and Brian turned back to her. "First Gerald, and now you. I'm going to need to find a place to work where all the good-looking, eligible men aren't gay."

Brian felt as though someone had pulled the rug from underneath him. His stomach clenched, and for a second he thought he might lose his lunch. Yes, he'd told a few people that he was gay—trusted people and close friends. Jesus, for a second he thought he could feel himself falling through the floor. Letting his head clear, he could tell she was teasing a little, and it was on the tip of his tongue to deny it, but he stopped himself. He was gay and he'd told Nicolai he wasn't ashamed of who he was, and he wasn't going to lie about it.

"I'm sorry, I shouldn't have said anything," Jeanie said. "That was inappropriate and none of my business." She looked embarrassed and uncomfortable.

"That's probably true, but since you brought it up, how could you tell?" Brian was a bit surprised and wondered how transparent he'd been acting. The butterflies in his stomach abated, and he felt his feet under him again.

"It's the way you looked at him, like he was the most important person in the world. Gerald looks at Dieter the exact same way whenever he comes into the office, and I'd give anything to have my husband look at me that way again. I think it's pretty wonderful. And to answer your next question, no, you don't have flames shooting out of your butt or anything. My brother's gay, so I guess I'm a little more tuned in." Her phone began to ring, and she turned her attention away from Brian, greeting the caller before transferring them.

"Thanks, Jeanie," he said with a relieved smile before realizing that his "secret" was going to be around the entire office in about ten seconds. Brian thought of asking her to keep it to herself, but that would only fan the flames. What was done was done. Everyone in the office had accepted Gerald without question. What did he really have to be afraid of? Leaving the reception area, Brian walked back to his office to get to work.

Brian spent much of the rest of the afternoon working on a number of his pending cases. He also asked one of the paralegals to draft a letter for Nicolai as a favor to him. A knock on his door pulled him out of the brief he'd been drafting. "There's a nasty rumor going through the office," Gerald said with a smile. "You big flamer."

"Took that long, did it?" Brian said before returning to his brief, not really wanting to think about this right now.

"Actually, I heard it hours ago, but decided to leave you alone," Gerald quipped before leaving him alone with the Rolle brief and his unsettled thoughts. Eventually, Brian forced himself to concentrate. He had plenty of work to do, and it needed to get done before he left the office.

Hours later, the office was quiet as Brian put the Rolle brief to bed. Rolling his neck, Brian was just about to get up and head home when his phone rang. Checking the display, he grabbed the phone when he saw his home number, wondering what was wrong.

"You'll never believe the conversation I had with your sister today," his mother began without preamble. "She told me she's a *lesbian.*" She actually whispered the last word as though it were dirty or something. "Then she insisted that she had to take care of Zoe, so I came with her." She sounded proud of herself for some reason.

"I'm just packing up here. I'll be home shortly." Brian didn't know what else to say, but he wasn't letting Georgia take the heat from their mother alone. Gathering his papers, he shoved them in his bag and took off for the elevator. It had been one hell of a day, and he knew it was going to get much worse. Pressing the button to call the elevator, his phone jangled in his pocket with a text message from Nicolai.

> *It was very sweet of you to help me today.*
>
> *Thank you.*

Brian loved how Nicolai spelled out the words instead of using the shortcuts. It made the note seem more personal and special, and he could almost hear Nicolai's deep voice saying the words to him. The elevator doors opened, and Brian stepped inside, pressing the floor for the parking garage.

You're welcome, he typed, and he was about to add that he'd see him this weekend, but stopped. For Nicolai, text messages were more than a convenient way to send a note—they were a vital method of communication, almost as important as a telephone call to a hearing person.

> *My mother just called and she's having a fit*
> *because Georgia came out to her today. I am on*
> *my way home. I'll message you later.*

Brian hit send as the elevator doors slid open on his floor. Walking to his car, Brian stopped outside the driver's-side door and began another message.

> *I think I am going to tell my mother about me.*

Brian hit send and then opened his car door and got inside.

The drive was mercifully short, with surprisingly little traffic. Brian had expected to receive a reply from Nicolai, but his phone remained silent. It worried him a little, but he had bigger things to deal with. He knew if he didn't hear from Nicolai soon, he'd try again. Pulling into the garage, Brian grabbed his case and got out of the car, walking into the house. He half expected to hear yelling, but all he heard was the sound of Zoe's video game drifting down the stairs. Walking through the house, he found his mother sitting alone in the living room.

"Thank goodness you're here."

"Where's Zoe?" Brian asked, cutting off what he was sure was going to be one of his mother's tirades.

"She's playing video games with Georgia. I wasn't sure I should leave them alone together, but with me in the house…." Her voice trailed off, and Brian felt his head throb as he glared at his mother. She stood up and began walking toward the stairs.

"No, Mom. Leave them alone. I think you and I need to talk," Brian said, and he motioned for his mother to sit down. She lowered herself onto the edge of the sofa, like she was ready to leap to the rescue at the slightest noise from upstairs. "First, let's get one thing straight. I am raising Zoe in a loving, accepting home. Georgia being a lesbian is completely irrelevant."

"But what if she—" his mother began and then stopped.

"How can you even think that? Georgia is your daughter, and after she came out to you and trusted you with something special about herself, all you can think about is that she might molest your granddaughter?" Brian gave her his most disgusted look. "I knew you'd have a problem with this."

"You knew?" She looked heartbroken for some reason.

"Yes. She came out to me a while ago," Brian said, and he wondered if he should tell her about himself. On his way home, he'd decided to tell her, but he wondered if now was the right time. Really, there would probably never be a right time, so he simply forged ahead. "Actually, Mom, we sort of came out to each other." Brian waited and let what he'd said kick in. He saw the second she realized what he'd said. Her mouth fell open, and he saw her eyes water. "Neither of us wanted to hurt you."

His mother stood up and walked toward the bottom of the stairs. "Zoe," she snapped. "Pack some clothes for tomorrow, you're coming home with me."

"Mother," Brian said firmly as he heard Zoe's footsteps on the stairs. "Zoe isn't going anywhere. It's a school night."

"She can't stay here with you," she hissed.

"Get back in the living room now, or get out of my house," Brian hissed between teeth clenched so tight his jaw hurt. "I mean it." Brian was shaking he was so angry. His mother's eyes widened, and Brian saw her conviction falter for just a second. Brian held her gaze, and she whirled around. For a short, petite woman, his mother could create quite a stir when she wanted to, and Brian felt every one of her footsteps as she stalked back into the living room.

Zoe walked slowly down the stairs, apprehension in every movement of her body. "What's wrong with Grandma and Aunt Georgia? They won't talk to each other, and Grandma looks like she's mad."

"Your grandma had a bit of a shock, but she's not mad at you. I got some of your favorite chicken nuggets and juice boxes when I went to the store. I'll make you some dinner once I calm your grandma down and get her to go home."

"Am I going with her? She said...." Zoe pointed to where his mother sat brooding on the sofa.

"No. You can visit on the weekend if you want, but you have school tomorrow and homework to finish tonight. Go into the kitchen and get a small snack until dinner."

"Can I have string cheese?" Zoe asked.

"Yes. One, and a juice box," Brian told her, and she hurried into the kitchen. The refrigerator door opened and closed. Soon Zoe ran by him in a blur, back up the stairs. "I said one juice box," Brian warned.

"This one's for Aunt Georgia," she explained with an adorable smile that Brian could never argue with. Brian nodded his approval, and she disappeared upstairs. Turning around, he walked toward the living room; it was time to face his mother.

"Is Zoe ready to go?" his mother asked as soon as Brian walked into the living room.

"Zoe is not going anywhere," Brian answered firmly before sitting down across from where she stood.

"Your father and I will not allow our granddaughter to stay in a house with... with deviants and...."

"Don't you say another word!" Brian retorted firmly. "Now sit down, and we can talk, or you can go home. But if you walk out that door," Brian said, pointing dramatically, "you will never see your granddaughter again!" Brian didn't make the threat lightly, but he saw his mother flinch and then she sat down. "Now, as I've told you, I'm gay. But that does not mean I'm some sort of deviant, and it certainly doesn't mean you suddenly get to take my daughter. So get that through your head now. If you want to talk, I'll be happy to explain what I can, but quite frankly I don't know much except what I feel."

His mother looked confused and took a while before she spoke. "But you were married," she said softly, some of her fight slipping away.

Brian sighed and wondered how he could explain. He decided on the plain truth. "I got Barbara pregnant and I married her because it was the right thing to do. We were never truly happy, at least I wasn't, but I was faithful for the entire time we were married. It was Barbara who cheated; I didn't." Brian could tell he really wasn't getting through, so he tried another tack. This was much harder than he'd expected. Yes, he'd known his mother would be upset and probably closed-minded, but he hadn't imagined it would be so tough for him to explain. He used words every day, made his living with them, and right now he couldn't find the words for this. "Mom, when we were kids, you always said that the thing you wanted most was for us to be happy. Did you mean that?"

"Of course I did," she answered firmly and quickly.

"Then what if that happiness means something that you find hard to understand? Are we still your children? Do you and Dad still love us, both of us?" Brian asked softly, figuring that a soft voice would carry more weight than a shout.

"But it's wrong."

"Not for me, and not for Georgia. Being gay is part of who we are. You don't have to be happy about it, but you do have to accept it." The doorbell rang, followed by a knock, as Brian finished his thought. Getting up, he wondered who else could be visiting. Walking to the door, he opened it and saw Nicolai standing on his doorstep, smiling at him.

"I came because I thought you might need some support," Nicolai said. "What you're doing is hard, and I wanted you to know you weren't alone."

Brian swallowed and motioned Nicolai inside.

"Who is at the door?" he heard his mother ask.

"A friend," Brian answered and saw the questioning look on Nicolai's face. Brian mouthed "Mother," and Nicolai nodded. Brian motioned toward the living room and heard Zoe call something from upstairs. "I have to see what Zoe wants," he explained to Nicolai, and Nicolai nodded his understanding. Brian hurried upstairs to find out what Zoe wanted. Once he got into the television room, he saw her and Georgia having some sort of tickle fight, with Zoe squealing her delight and trying to squirm away.

As soon as she saw him, Georgia stopped and looked at him. "How's Mom?"

"I got her calmed down for both of us," Brian explained. "We'll talk after she goes and Zoe's in bed." Georgia nodded, and Brian grabbed Zoe, twirling her around to more laughter and happiness before setting her down. He had to get downstairs before his mother did something to Nicolai. "I'll make dinner soon," he promised.

"I'm okay, Daddy," Zoe said as she knelt down to turn on her Wii, challenging Aunt Georgia to some sort of dancing death match. Brian watched the two of them start their game before leaving the room and going down the stairs. Approaching the living room, he heard Nicolai's voice, deep and soft, drift to his ears, followed by his mother's.

"Is there something I did wrong to make them this way?" he heard his mother ask, and Brian stopped moving. They were talking, and his mother seemed to be asking things. The idea had never occurred to Brian, but he should have known. There was no way anyone could deny Nicolai anything. Brian knew he couldn't, the man was so sweet and disarming. Backing up, Brian left the hall and went through the dining room to the kitchen, deciding to let the two of them talk.

In the kitchen, Brian quietly tried to make dinner. It had been awhile since he'd managed to mess up reheating frozen food, so he set some of Zoe's chicken nuggets on a cookie sheet and turned on the oven. Once it had warmed up, he placed the chicken inside and turned on the timer before going in to rescue Nicolai. When Brian walked into the living room, he could barely believe his eyes. His mother, or as he thought of her, the dragon lady, was sitting on the sofa, listening intently to Nicolai as he held her hands. It was an almost endearing sight, and one he never thought he'd see. If he lived to be a hundred, he'd never stop being amazed by Nicolai's perception. "Is everything okay?"

His mother looked at him, and Brian saw Nicolai follow her gaze, then his face brightened into a smile that Brian knew was just for him. His mother stood up and let go of Nicolai's hands before walking to Brian. "I think I understand a little better now," she told him before retrieving her coat from the back of one of the chairs. "Tell your sister to call me."

Brian nodded slowly, his eyes wide in surprise, as she left the house. "What did you tell her?" Brian asked after he'd turned to Nicolai.

"Sometimes it is easier to speak with someone who isn't your child," Nicolai said slowly.

"You're not going to tell me, are you?"

Nicolai shook his head as an answer and grinned at him. Not that Brian minded. Whatever got his mother off the warpath was a good thing. Brian didn't ask any more questions—he simply walked closer to Nicolai, his eyes locking on Nicolai's. "Zoe and Georgia are upstairs," he mouthed, and Nicolai nodded. Brian saw him swallow as Brian moved still closer. "I want you," Brian signed, trying to remember each of the signs as he moved still closer. At the first touch, Brian felt Nicolai shiver, and as he pulled him closer, Nicolai's eyes widened, but he made no move to back away, and his eyes never left Brian's. "Sometimes I wonder how you can understand me so well."

"I understand you just fine," Nicolai said.

"Do you understand that if Zoe and Georgia weren't here, I'd go all caveman and take you upstairs to make love to you until you could hear yourself scream, even if you are deaf?"

Nicolai didn't answer him, but Brian felt him shiver, and he felt Nicolai's excitement press back against him. Brian wanted to whisper soft, sweet things in Nicolai's ear, but he knew that wouldn't do, so he moved his hand along the side of Nicolai's cheek, tracing his finger around Nicolai's ear.

"*Ding,*" rang from the kitchen, and Brian thought it appropriate because Nicolai was making part of him stand up and go ding. Brian stepped back just before Zoe scrambled quickly down the stairs.

Zoe ran up to Nicolai, hugging him as she signed hello. "I've been learning," Zoe said, and then she proceeded to ruin Brian's surprise by showing him all the things she could say now. Nicolai watched everything she showed him.

"What's burning?" Georgia asked as she came down the stairs, and Brian rushed to the kitchen to pull what remained of Zoe's chicken nuggets out of the oven. Slapping the tray onto the burners, Brian glared at the black lumps before picking up the phone to order a pizza, which was exactly what he should have done anyway.

"I met your boyfriend," Georgia said as she entered the kitchen, just before she began to laugh. "You definitely need someone else to do the cooking." Georgia continued laughing, and Brian glared at her until he, too, began to chuckle.

"I ordered a pizza," Brian explained, motioning to his sister. "So what did you think?"

"Brian, if I were into boys, I'd steal that man away from you. He's adorably sweet, and Zoe seems to like him." Georgia leaned over and gave him a kiss on the cheek. "I have to go, but thanks for taking the heat with Mom."

"That was Nicolai. I don't know what he said to her, but she changed her tune, or at least seemed a lot less hostile. Mom even tried to take Zoe with her," Brian explained.

"That's Mom. She knows everything about everything, and it's her way or the highway. I have to go because I still have studying to do, but I love you, bro."

"Same here," Brian told her before giving her a hug. "Maybe we can get together for lunch or dinner so you can get to know Nicolai better."

"He's important to you, isn't he?" Georgia shook her head. "Don't answer that question. You don't want to jinx it." Georgia grinned devilishly. "I'll see you later." She breezed out of the kitchen, and while he was scraping the chicken nuggets into the trash, he heard the front door close.

"Daddy, I'm hungry," Zoe said from the doorway, Nicolai trailing behind her as he held her hand.

"I ordered a pizza," Brian said, making sure he was looking at Nicolai. "Would you stay for dinner?"

"Please," Zoe asked, but Nicolai couldn't hear her. Brian nodded to her, and she turned around and signed.

Nicolai nodded and signed, "Thank you."

"Zoe. You need to finish your homework. You can do it in the living room if you want, but I need to see it before you go to bed."

"Okay," Zoe answered, hurrying out of the room to get her bag.

"Where did Zoe learn those signs?" Nicolai asked.

"That was supposed to be a surprise. She and I have been taking classes at the Institute for the Deaf. I know reading lips is harder for you."

"You did that for me?"

"Yes, and for Zoe and myself. I wanted to be able to communicate with you. It's going to take some time, but I thought it important." Brian swallowed, realizing just how close he was to voicing his feelings, and he wasn't sure Nicolai was ready for that. If he were truthful with himself, he wasn't sure if he was ready yet.

Brian double-checked that they were alone before catching Nicolai's eye once again. Zoe had a way of entering a room like a hurricane, and what he wanted to say was for Nicolai only. "This weekend we had planned to spend Saturday afternoon together and then have dinner. I'd like to ask you to stay for breakfast on Sunday morning." Brian stroked Nicolai's cheek and felt the other man lean into the touch. He was falling for Nicolai, Brian could feel it, and he was happier than he could ever remember being with Barbara, though he'd only known him a little over a month. The words were on the tip of his tongue, but he stopped himself yet again.

"What about Zoe?"

"She's going to be with her mother this weekend."

"No. Have you told her?"

Brian shook his head. "I will. I need to give myself a little time. I just told my mother, and everyone in the office knows. I'll tell Zoe soon, but it's something she and I need to talk about together."

"Is there something that worries you?" Nicolai was so insightful that Brian shouldn't have been surprised that he'd picked up on Brian's reservations.

"I'm not sure quite how to tell her. She's asked about Georgia, and I was able to answer her. But there's a difference between explaining being gay in general and telling your nine-year-old daughter that her father is gay. I know this is my worry, and that she'll be okay with it. I also know that she'll tell her mother." Nicolai got this look that Brian couldn't read, and it made his stomach jump nervously. "I know. I'm a bit of a coward."

"You're not a coward. She could make trouble for you and for Zoe. Neither of you deserve that," Nicolai said, and Brian knew he was trying to be understanding.

"I'm not ashamed of you, and I will tell her next week. I promise."

"Just be honest with her when you do. She understands and sees a lot more than you think," Nicolai told him. "Your daughter is a very intelligent and special child," he said as he signed.

"Daddy, come see what I drew," Zoe called from the other room.

Brian let his arms fall to his side. He knew Nicolai was right. Motioning Nicolai through to the other room, they both admired the picture Zoe had drawn of Nicolai. "I had to draw the picture of a friend, so I drew you," she explained, forgetting to look at Nicolai, and Brian relayed the message as best he could, then he saw the huge smile on Nicolai's face. The doorbell rang, and Brian grabbed his wallet before answering the door to get their dinner.

SATURDAY morning, Brian slept in a lot later than usual. Opening his eyes, he turned toward his alarm clock and saw it was already after ten. Brian would have hoped that the first thought that popped into his head was one of Nicolai, but instead a conversation with Barbara from the evening before ran through his head, sending a shiver through him.

The conversation started like so many he'd had with her in the past year, but the tone had been different last night.

"I need more money, Brian. I can barely live on what you're giving me now," she'd said, almost before Brian had a chance to close the door behind her. Since he got the house, one of the things his lawyer had recommended was having the locks changed, and Brian was eternally grateful for that advice because Barbara would simply walk in as though she owned it.

"I'm sorry, but you need to find work. We've talked about this before, and I'm going to stick to what's in the agreement. I have contacts around town, I can put you in touch with people who can help you," Brian offered, as she slumped down onto the leather sofa. Barbara didn't look good. She obviously wasn't sleeping, and Brian wondered if she was drinking. He didn't smell alcohol, but she had the drawn look of someone who drank more than was good for them.

"You need to pay me more. I've been looking for work, and my lawyer says that as long as I'm trying to find work, you need to pay me the full amount," Barbara snapped, her heavy makeup looking almost garish. When they were married, Barbara had always looked her best, but now she looked like she'd half tried and given up.

"I'm not the unemployment office, and I highly doubt your lawyer would tell you something that ridiculous. You need to get yourself together. Find a job and find someone to make you happy."

Barbara's eyes, which had been drooping closed, popped open, and she looked at him like she was seeing something new. "You're dating someone, aren't you?" She leapt to her feet, almost stalking toward him. "You have been—I can see it on your face. That little smile you can't stop from showing." She half sneered as though she'd discovered some big secret.

"My personal life is none of your concern," Brian explained. "I can date if I wish and see whom I wish. I'm not the one who was doing it during our marriage." Brian couldn't help getting a dig in, and it shut her up, which was the desired effect.

Zoe rushed down the stairs carrying her bag. She dropped it and leapt into his arms, giving him a huge hug. "I'll see you later, Daddy. Don't be lonely while I'm gone."

"I won't, honey," he reassured her, and heard Barbara mutter something that sounded like "I'll bet." "You have a good time with your mother, and I'll see you Sunday." He put Zoe down, and she pulled open the door before rushing outside into the blisteringly cold evening.

"If I catch you doing anything, I'll bring it to my lawyer and the judge," Barbara warned him with a scowl before turning to leave the house, closing the door with a resounding thud behind her.

Barbara's words kept playing in his head, and they wouldn't stop. He knew her legal threats were ridiculous. Yes, she could cause trouble for him, but mostly she could only do her best to make his life miserable. That wasn't what bothered him, so much as the way she'd said it. Week after week, his ex-wife became increasingly bitter and determined that Brian owed her something. He'd taken care of her while they were married and offered her a fair settlement afterward. He knew now he'd never loved her and that getting married had probably been a mistake, but at the time he'd thought it was the honorable thing to do.

"Who would have known," he said softly to the room before pushing back the covers and getting out of bed. He had a date with Nicolai today, and they were going to spend the night together. That left him both excited and a little nervous. Padding to the bathroom, Brian looked at himself in the mirror, wondering if Nicolai would like what he saw. He wasn't ugly, he knew that, but years of working hard had left little time for exercise, and Brian poked his stomach a few times before sighing and reaching for the shaving cream.

His morning went by slowly, with Brian looking at the clock every five minutes. He tried watching television and gave up, turning it off. He straightened up the house and ran the vacuum cleaner, even tackling Zoe's media/playroom upstairs. Realizing he was simply wasting time, Brian sent Nicolai a text message and received a quick reply. Grabbing his coat, Brian hurried to the garage and got into his car. Opening the overhead door, he slowly backed out of the snow-covered driveway and made his way through the streets in a light snow.

As he pulled up in front of the house, Brian saw the curtains flutter, and soon the front door opened. Nicolai carried a small bag, stowing it in the trunk before getting into the warm car.

"I need to get some wine, and I thought we could grab a nice light lunch first at—" Brian faltered, knowing there was no way Nicolai would understand him. Lifting his hand, Brian spelled out "La Boulangerie" with his fingers, and Nicolai chuckled at him as he nodded his head before leaning over the seat expectantly. Brian met him halfway, receiving a light, sweet kiss before putting the car in gear and pulling away from the curb.

"I made an appointment in Chicago at the Art Institute," Nicolai told him as they left their last stop, Sommelier Wines, before heading to Brian's house for the evening. "They seemed anxious to meet with me and agreed to provide a sign-language interpreter," Nicolai said when they reached the car.

"Good. The Clerk of Courts has confirmed the date for the appeals hearing, so I'll make a hotel reservation for us."

"What about Zoe? Will she go too?"

"No. She has school, so she will stay with my parents. My mother will see that she gets to and from school." Since her little talk with Nicolai, she'd been bending over backward to help him, and Georgia had even remarked that she seemed almost accepting.

They lapsed into quiet while Brian drove. It was funny, but when Nicolai was in the car, he never so much as turned on the radio, almost as if since Nicolai couldn't hear it, he shouldn't, either. As he drove, he realized there were a lot of things he did differently when Nicolai was around. He didn't listen to music or watch television. The few times he had turned it on, he'd been sure to turn on the closed captioning. He hadn't even realized he'd done it until now, but he removed all unnecessary sounds when Nicolai was around.

"You can turn on the radio if you want," Nicolai told him, but Brian only nodded and took Nicolai's hand in his as they rode down the freeway. It wasn't necessary. He would have told Nicolai that having him with him was plenty, but he didn't, instead he let his hand communicate what was important.

By the time they arrived at the house, it was snowing hard, and Brian pulled into the garage, closing the door on what was probably becoming a blizzard. Getting Nicolai's bag, he unlocked the door and hung up their coats before motioning Nicolai to the living room. Brian hurried up the stairs and placed the bag in his room before returning to where Nicolai waited for him.

"Do you want me to make dinner?" Nicolai said with an expression that told Brian he was thinking about the untimely death of those chicken nuggets.

"No," Brian explained. "One of the clients I helped a few months ago is a chef, and he made dinner and left specific instructions for reheating it. You can help if you want, though," Brian said carefully before leaning forward to capture Nicolai's lips with his own. As he pulled back, Nicolai followed, his arms slinking around Brian's neck as he continued kissing him. Brian made a low, guttural sound, heedless of the fact that Nicolai couldn't hear it. He simply couldn't keep it in. But what surprised him were the little sounds Nicolai made as they kissed. Brian figured Nicolai had no idea he was making them, and that made them that much more exciting because it was an uncensored show of pleasure. About two seconds from forgetting dinner and taking Nicolai upstairs, Brian broke the kiss before holding Nicolai tight, letting the warmth of their bodies mingle.

"Let's make dinner and then we can make love," Brian said, looking deep into Nicolai's eyes before taking his hand and leading him toward the kitchen. Brian got Nicolai making the salad while he put the containers Dominic had left into the oven and set the timer according to the chef's detailed instructions. He even showed them to Nicolai just to make sure. While Nicolai finished the salad, Brian set the dining-room table with his best dishes and even managed to find a pair of candlesticks and candles, setting them in the center of the table before lighting them. He wanted everything to be as special as he could. Lowering the lighting, Brian went back into the kitchen, handing the dressing Dominic had left to Nicolai for him to toss with the salad.

Once it was done, he carried the bowl into the dining room, and the timer dinged on the stove. Hurrying back, he pulled out the dishes and carried them into the dining room as well, placing the hot dishes on trivets. Once everything was ready, he led Nicolai out of the kitchen and into the dining room, showing him to his seat right across from his. Then Brian poured them each a glass of wine, filling the plates and setting out one for each of them. He'd eaten with Nicolai and he always felt this need to talk, even if Nicolai couldn't hear, but not tonight. There was nothing to say that wouldn't be said much better later when it was just the two of them, upstairs, alone.

So they ate, quietly and slowly, touching hands every few bites, sharing a glance or a smile. Brian kept expecting a knock on the door or an emergency telephone call of some sort, but nothing came. He could hear the wind howling around the house and see snow blowing by the windows, but inside it was warm, and Brian could feel it all the way to his heart.

When their plates were empty, Brian took the dishes to the kitchen, motioning lightly for Nicolai to stay where he was. Brian made sure the dishes were in the sink and everything was turned off. Then he returned to the dining room, blew out the candles, and turned off the lights before taking Nicolai's hand and leading him up the stairs and down the hallway to his bedroom.

Turning on a small light, Brian sat on the edge of the bed, looking at Nicolai as he stood in front of him. "I'm nervous and inexperienced at this," Brian admitted, and Nicolai's eyes widened. Brian almost expected Nicolai to balk or think he was some sort of freak, but Nicolai's expression softened, and he leaned toward Brian, kissing him softly at first and then harder, pressing him back until Brian lay on the mattress, returning every kiss Nicolai gave. Brian didn't know what to do, so he followed Nicolai's lead, holding onto Nicolai as they kissed.

Brian jumped slightly when Nicolai's chilly fingers slid under his shirt and along his skin, but they soon warmed and then felt like brands against his skin, hot and driving him crazy. Brian had dreamed of being touched by another man for so long, he could almost believe that this was an illusion, but Nicolai's fingers lightly plucking at one of his nipples shattered any misconception in a spectacular way. Nicolai continued kissing even as his fingers worked the button of Brian's shirt, parting the fabric. Then Nicolai's lips slipped from his before kissing trails along his skin, hot wet lines that made Brian's stomach muscles flutter and his back arch, and when Nicolai's tongue teased around one of his nipples, Brian stopped thinking as instinct seemed to take over.

Rolling them on the bed, Brian lay on top of Nicolai, gazing down into his eyes as Nicolai's now-warm hands pressed to his chest.

"Let me," Nicolai said, but Brian wasn't sure. He'd always been in charge in the past, but he nodded slowly, and Nicolai slid his shirt off his shoulders before guiding him back onto the mattress. Brian watched every move Nicolai made as he lowered his head and began kissing his skin. Lips kissed along his shoulder, mouth and tongue working that spot at the base of his neck until Brian thought he couldn't take any more. Nicolai lifted Brian's arms above his head, admonishing him with his eyes when he tried to bring them down again. So he kept them there as Nicolai's tongue slid down his side, and he had to stop himself from squirming away from the delightful torture. Nicolai was driving him crazy, totally and completely crazy. His pants were way too tight, his cock straining against the fabric, throbbing so hard it ached. And Nicolai seemed in no hurry whatsoever to do anything about it. Instead, he kissed Brian's belly just above the waist of his pants, and Brian held his breath, wishing Nicolai would go lower. "Close your eyes," Nicolai told him, his voice even deeper than normal.

Brian wasn't sure he wanted to, but Nicolai's gaze seared right through him, and Brian nodded before letting his eyes drift closed. He was used to being in control, in the office, at home. But letting Nicolai have control here felt so right, so good, that he gave in and let his head rest back against the pillow as Nicolai's lips, hands, and tongue played his body like a fine instrument. Brian lost himself in the sensations, his hips bucking lightly, cock straining. A few times he thought he was going to come, and Nicolai hadn't even taken his pants off.

Brian held his breath as fingers finally worked at his belt. He didn't open his eyes, but he could hear his own voice in his head praying that Nicolai wouldn't stop. The waist of his pants parted and a gentle tap on his hip followed. Brian lifted his butt off the bed, and his pants slipped down his legs. Shoes thunked on the floor and then his pants were gone, his erection pulsing as Nicolai's hands stroked up his legs. Without thinking, Brian parted his legs, giving himself to Nicolai without reservation. Brian waited, hearing the sounds of shoes hitting the floor, then the jangle of a belt buckle, the soft but distinctive sound of pants being lowered over masculine legs, then fabric crumpling on the floor.

The bed dipped and shook beneath him, and Brian kept his eyes closed, waiting for what Nicolai would do. His breath caught in his throat, and he cried out, filling the room with sounds Nicolai couldn't hear, as Nicolai's hot tongue slid along his length. He tried to remember the last time he'd been touched this way and he couldn't. This was something that hadn't happened while he was married and.... "Oh... my... God!" Brian cried from deep in his lungs as Nicolai took him into his mouth. Opening his eyes, Brian lifted his head and saw Nicolai's lips sliding around his cock. That had to be one of the sexiest sights Brian had ever seen, and he almost came just from looking. With a soft groan, Brian lowered his arms, touching Nicolai's cheek lightly. He had to think of a way to communicate to him just what he was feeling. The simple touch seemed inadequate, but Nicolai seemed to understand, and Brian felt Nicolai's lips clamp hard around him, and he was sucked deep into his lover's hot mouth.

Sensation and excitement threatened to overwhelm him. Brian tightened his hands on the bedding as though he needed to anchor himself or he'd float away on the intense pleasure that was making his head spin. His legs shook, and warm hands pressed against his hips to still them as the last of Brian's control threatened to snap. Nicolai seemed to be encouraging it as he sucked harder, his tongue doing indescribable things. And to make matters worse, Nicolai made these deep, moaning sounds in his throat that drove Brian's passion even higher. Building pressure deep inside Brian threatened to carry him away, and he tapped Nicolai's arm to try to warn him, but the man simply sucked harder, pulling Brian's orgasm right out of him.

Brian knew he was screaming, his body shaking as he was propelled over the precipice of desire into a free-fall of bliss and total, utter, and complete euphoric nirvana. His body limp and pliant, Brian felt Nicolai's lips slide away, and then they were on his, kissing and probing as warm skin pressed to his. Chest to chest, legs entwining with his, Nicolai's weight pressed him into the mattress, and Brian grasped the opportunity to run his hands over

Nicolai's skin, the feel of his strong back, the curve of his butt, the way the hair on his chest tickled Brian's skin, but best of all was the slide of Nicolai's length against his hip, accompanied by his lover's needy little moans.

Kissing Nicolai hard, Brian feasted on his sweet lips as he felt Nicolai's body tense. Nicolai broke the kiss, throwing his head back, mouth open wide in a silent cry as Brian felt him climax between their bodies before collapsing back into Brian's arms, where he held and petted his amazing lover, who had already taken him to places Brian hadn't known existed. Brian had spent so much of his life denying who he was to himself and the rest of the world that it felt amazing to do something as simple as hold Nicolai in his arms, regardless of the great sex they'd just had.

Nicolai began to squirm slightly, and Brian released him, letting Nicolai recline on the mattress while Brian got off the bed and padded to the bathroom, returning with a warm cloth and towel. Cleaning off Nicolai's skin, Brian dried him and then cleaned himself before putting the towel and cloth back in the bathroom and joining Nicolai beneath the covers. He immediately tugged Nicolai close, letting them both get comfortable before turning out the light. Brian felt Nicolai moving for a few minutes, and then he seemed to get comfortable, and soon all Brian heard was the sound of his breathing. Too happy and excited to sleep, Brian lay awake for a long time, staring at the ceiling and listening to the small sounds Nicolai made as he slept. Eventually, Brian closed his eyes and let sleep overtake him, dreaming of having Nicolai all to himself for a few nights in Chicago.

CHAPTER 4

NICOLAI woke in a strange place, and it took him a few seconds before he remembered that he was in a Chicago hotel room with Brian, and why he'd woken. A familiar buzz shook near his head, and he reached to the nightstand for his phone so it wouldn't wake Brian. He hated to move, but it could be important. Looking around to make sure Brian was still asleep—he was, thankfully—Nicolai turned the phone away from his sleeping lover's eyes and pressed the button so he could view the message. He didn't recognize the number, so he displayed the message. It was yet another one from Justin. The man wouldn't leave him alone, and now he appeared to be using a different phone. Checking the time, Nicolai saw it was almost seven, and they had some time before they had to get up. Nicolai opened the actual message and pressed the delete button without responding or reading it before turning off the phone and rolling back into Brian's embrace, letting himself drift back to sleep.

Nicolai felt Brian move behind him, and he rolled over so he could see Brian's face. When he did, he saw Brian's mouth brighten to a smile and then he was being kissed. And before he knew it, Brian's weight shifted, pressing him into the mattress. Brian didn't try to talk or communicate when they made love, other than with his body, which Nicolai really appreciated. Justin had always spoken to him and expected Nicolai to read his lips, even in the height of passion. At times like those, Nicolai had much better things to do than try to read lips. Brian instinctively seemed to understand that.

Hell, Brian seemed to understand a lot of things where he was concerned, and he really seemed to understand Nicolai's needs without treating him like there was something wrong with him.

Tapping Brian on the shoulder, Nicolai waited for him to look into his eyes before pointing toward the clock next to the hotel bed. He really wanted to make love, regardless of the fact that they'd made love all evening and well into the night. Brian had seemed nervous and jumpy about his appearance in front of the appellate court, and Nicolai had made it his mission to try to make him forget for as long as possible. He saw a very particular expression cross Brian's face, which he now knew was his "I don't want to get up yet, but I have to" face. After another kiss and a tight hug, Brian's warmth slid away, and Nicolai watched as he padded naked to the bathroom, paying particular attention to Brian's bouncy butt before it disappeared behind the bathroom door. They had yet to broach that particular area in their sex lives, and Nicolai had been reluctant to press, for many reasons. Not that he was in any particular hurry— the sex had been amazing.

The bathroom door opened and light spilled into the room. In the crescent of light, Nicolai saw Brian crook his little finger, a wry smile on his face. Getting out of the warm bed, Nicolai walked into the bathroom to see Brian climbing into the shower, a "come hither" look on his face.

After an amazing shower, they dressed quickly so Nicolai wouldn't be late for his appointment at the Art Institute. He and Brian met Gerald and Dieter in the café off the lobby of the art deco hotel for breakfast. Nicolai got something quick to eat, and after kissing Brian good-bye, hurried out of the hotel.

Normally, Nicolai would have walked, but the wind off the lake was bitterly cold, and he would be late if he didn't get there fast, so he hailed a cab and handed the driver a slip of paper with his destination written on it. From experience, he'd learned it was easier that way. The driver let him off in front of the museum, and Nicolai walked around to the back, entering a nondescript door that led to the administrative offices. Nicolai told the security guard his name and sat down. When the man tried to tell him something, Nicolai told him he was deaf, and the guard nodded and signaled for him to wait a minute. Nicolai didn't wait long before a tall woman walked through the door, signing to him. Nicolai returned the greeting, and she motioned for him to follow her.

Nicolai spent the next two hours discussing his proposal with the Art Institute's glass-arts curator and got a close-up tour of the windows in question. They were spectacular, the cobalt blue surprisingly warm and rich, not cold at all, like most blues. They always reminded Nicolai of warm, tropical water. When they were finished, the curator thanked Nicolai for coming in and told him they would let him know in the next few weeks if his proposal had been accepted.

There were small, telltale signs that Nicolai had long ago noticed—the way they looked at him, when peoples' eyes dilated, small changes in facial skin tone, the tiny crinkles around the eyes, and a certain gut reaction told him he'd most likely be getting a call sooner than that. Hyped and excited, Nicolai caught a cab to the federal courthouse. Brian's hearing was scheduled to start in a little less than half an hour, and he could just about make it if he were lucky.

The cab driver must have thought he was at Indianapolis because he wove through traffic and got Nicolai to the courthouse in what must have been record time. Nicolai paid the driver and got out of the cab, happy he still had his breakfast, before walking into the courthouse. He had no idea where to go, so he made his way to the Clerk of Courts Office and through some miracle, the woman behind the desk was patient, writing her answers down so Nicolai could find the appropriate courtroom.

Checking his watch, Nicolai realized he had five minutes, so he pulled open the door slowly and saw Brian and Gerald sitting in the front of the room. Looking around, he saw Dieter sitting on one of the benches, so Nicolai joined him. Nicolai had never been in a courtroom before, and he looked around. People came in from the back of the room, and everyone stood. The appellate panel of judges took their seats, and everyone sat.

Since he couldn't hear what was being said, Nicolai watched the judges very carefully, every motion, noticing every movement of their facial muscles. Nicolai wasn't personally involved in this case, but Dieter had become one of his dearest friends, and Nicolai could feel Dieter's nervousness rolling off him. He knew what this case meant to Dieter.

Dieter had told him how his great-grandfather and his grandmother had fled Austria ahead of the Nazis with only what they could carry. The five paintings involved in the lawsuit had supposedly been left to the Belvedere by his great-grandmother, but they'd been able to prove that the purported bequest wasn't valid. Dieter had told him that the case now revolved around the fact that they were suing the Austrians in US court because the Belvedere made money on the paintings in the United States.

Nicolai had asked why they didn't sue in Austria, and Dieter had explained that in order to bring suit there, he would have to put up a bond equal to the value of the paintings. They'd won in the lower court, but the Austrians were appealing on the grounds of national sovereignty. Dieter's story really tugged at Nicolai's heart. His family had fled the Nazis as well as the Soviets, and like Dieter's family, they'd had to leave everything behind. So the thought of Dieter getting his family legacy back felt like a win for him and everyone who'd lost everything and had to start over. To top it off, Nicolai tended to be competitive in nature, and he wanted Brian to win. So at that particular moment, Dieter wasn't the only nervous person sitting on that particular bench.

Reaching over, Nicolai took Dieter's hand to help calm his friend's nerves as he waited to see what would happen. He saw the judges talking, and he could make out that each lawyer would have thirty minutes to present their case. The panel would then ask questions. Nicolai watched as the judge who appeared to be in charge turned to the other lawyer, who then stood up. Nicolai could not make out what he was saying, so he looked at the judges to watch their reaction.

Nicolai knew they worked hard to school their reactions, but even the smallest twinge of an eyebrow registered on Nicolai's radar. Once the lawyer was done, the judges asked their questions, but Nicolai could only see the judge's questions and gauge their reaction to the answers. To Nicolai, they didn't seem particularly impressed. Then he watched as Brian stood up. He really wished he knew what he was saying, but as he watched, he could see that the nerves Brian had expressed having appeared to be gone. He looked confident and stood tall, and to Nicolai's eyes, the judges seemed to wake up and were listening attentively. Their eyes looked brighter, and they sat just a little straighter in their chairs. Granted, Nicolai knew that might not mean anything other than they were shifting in their seats. Nicolai turned to Dieter and smiled at him, getting a confused smile in return. Obviously being able to hear what was going on wasn't much help, either.

Nicolai continued watching as Brian finished speaking and the questions began. Nicolai watched, and he felt Dieter tensing up next to him. He wasn't sure why, but Nicolai kept a close watch on every expression from the judges. Finally, Brian sat down.

"Is that it?" Nicolai asked as softly as he could into Dieter's ear and saw the other man nod just before everyone stood up and the judges left the room. Nicolai remained standing as he watched Brian pack up his papers before he and Gerald walked to where they waited. The other attorneys filed by, and then the four of them were alone. Brian led the way out, and the rest of them followed.

"Let's get some lunch and we can talk," Brian suggested, looking at Nicolai. He could see Brian was still excited, but there was something else in his expression that worried Nicolai, and he was anxious to find out what Brian was thinking.

Nicolai felt Brian's hand on his back, lightly guiding him out of the courthouse and onto the cold, windy street. They didn't stay there long before Brian led them into what looked like a nice restaurant. Nicolai saw Brian talk to the hostess, and then they were being led to a booth. Brian motioned for him to slide in first, and then he sat next to him. Nicolai kept looking to Brian for some clue of how he thought things had gone, but Brian didn't say anything. Finally, Nicolai saw Dieter break the ice.

"Do you think it went well?" Dieter asked from across the table. Nicolai could tell he was still nervous—the obvious clue was his leg bouncing under the table.

Nicolai looked to Brian, hoping for an answer.

"I really don't know. They asked a lot of good questions, but that doesn't mean much," Brian said.

"I thought they seemed much more interested in what you had to say than what the other attorneys said," Nicolai offered, and he was a little shocked at Brian's expression. "You don't have to hear what people are saying to know how they're reacting to something," Nicolai added defensively, a little upset that his lover apparently discounted his opinion that easily.

Brian's expression softened. "I'm sorry. I know you see things other people don't." Brian took his hand beneath the table. "Would you tell us what you saw?"

Nicolai was tempted to remain quiet, but didn't want to act childish. "All three judges were bored when the defendant's lawyer was speaking," Nicolai explained, keeping his speech slow and measured, hoping that he wasn't speaking too loud. "But as you spoke, they sat taller in their chairs, and their eyes seemed brighter. I know it sounds dumb, but they were more alert, even if they weren't trying to look it. There are some things you can't hide, even when you want to."

"That doesn't mean they'll rule in our favor," Brian explained.

"No," Nicolai agreed, speaking to Brian. "But it does mean they were intrigued and weren't dismissing your argument out of hand. It's good, I think."

"Yes, it is," Brian told him, his face moving a little closer. "I should not have dismissed your observations. I won't do it again," Nicolai saw Brian say, and he smiled and nodded. Then he saw Brian look away, and he followed his lover's gaze to the server. Nicolai showed Brian what he wanted to eat and drink and let Brian order for him. It was easier that way. Nicolai knew his speech was better than most, but especially in crowded restaurants, servers often had trouble understanding him.

"What happens next?" Nicolai saw Dieter ask.

"We wait," Brian answered, making sure to look at him. "The court could rule in our favor, remand the case back to the lower court, or throw out our judgment altogether. All we can do is wait." Brian looked resigned.

"How long?" Nicolai asked, and he saw Brian shrug. Their drinks arrived, and Brian lifted his glass. The others did as well, and Nicolai looked to Brian for an explanation, but none came. After touching glasses, which Nicolai had always thought was strange, they drank. As usual, he didn't try to follow the entire conversation. His neck would get tired, so he watched Brian and tried to follow along as best he could.

After eating a wonderful lunch, they left the restaurant and took a cab back to the hotel. Brian had already checked out and placed their bags in the trunk of his car. He said good-bye to Dieter and Gerald before getting into the car.

The ride home took a while, with Nicolai sitting and watching the scenery pass outside the window. When they arrived at his house, Nicolai got out of the car.

"Can you come in?" Nicolai asked, and Brian didn't answer right away. Nicolai always hated when their time together came to an end. They texted and e-mailed, but he only really got to see Brian for any length of time every other weekend, when Zoe was with her mother. Nicolai understood the reasons, but that didn't mean he had to be happy about them, and he wasn't ready to let Brian go quite yet. But he wasn't about to beg, either. Brian had to decide the priorities in his life.

"My mother will be bringing Zoe home after dinner," Brian said as he moved closer, and Nicolai lifted his suitcase before walking toward the front door. He felt a hand on his and then Brian lifted away the suitcase, holding it for him.

Nicolai unlocked and pushed open the door. He knew immediately that something wasn't right. Stepping inside, he looked to Brian as he followed him and closed the door. "What's wrong?" he saw Brian ask.

"Not sure. Something feels wrong," Nicolai said before wandering from room to room. Nothing seemed out of place, but he couldn't get rid of the feeling that someone had been here while he was gone. He could see nothing, and even when he looked into his backyard, he didn't see tracks in the snow, but he couldn't shake that feeling. "It must be my imagination," Nicolai said after he'd placed his suitcase in his bedroom.

"Will this make you feel better?" Brian moved closer before taking him into his arms. The kiss was instantly hard and deep, Brian's tongue probing and tasting Nicolai's mouth, and he gave himself over to his lover's passion. Brian moved them toward the sofa, and they fell together, with Brian continuing to kiss him before lifting his shirt.

Nicolai had found that Brian was fascinated with his nipples, so it was no surprise that he felt first Brian's fingers plucking them, then when their kiss ended, Brian licked and sucked one then the other. Nicolai arched his back and thrust forward for more. He loved the way Brian seemed to care for him. He had no idea how Brian knew just what he liked. Nicolai knew he never talked when they made love, and he'd tried to remind himself to ask him, but the only time he thought about it was when Brian was doing these amazing things to him. And that was so not the time. Especially since Brian's lips kissed a trail down his stomach, and Nicolai felt the loop on his belt open and the zipper of his pants slip down. The fabric parted, and then Brian yanked his pants down past his hips.

"Brian," he said. Nicolai wasn't even sure if he'd said anything out loud, but he felt Brian's lips on him, taking him in, and the breath whooshed from his lungs. He loved it when Brian used his lips on him. He might not have had much experience, but Brian was a fast learner, and in a few weeks, he'd become a freaking expert. Especially when he….

Nicolai's mind shut off as Brian took him deep. He felt his eyes cross and tried to catch his breath but failed. Lifting his head, Nicolai had to watch. He had to see what Brian was doing to him, and the sight of his cock sliding past Brian's perfect lips, his eyes looking up at him, filled with such feeling, nearly made Nicolai lose it right there. Brian slid his lips away and said something to him, but Nicolai couldn't make it out through his watery eyes. Then he felt Brian settling him fully onto the cushions, making sure he was comfortable before sucking him hard, fingers plucking at his nipples. Nicolai was swept away to a state of heavenly bliss where all his nerves fired at the same time, sending waves of pleasure up and down his body. Everywhere Brian touched him with his hands or his mouth, he came alive. His legs shook and his arms quivered as he rode the waves of pleasure.

Pressure built deep inside, beginning at his heart and radiating outward in every direction, until he could contain it no longer. Nicolai's head flopped back against the cushions, and his mouth opened as he came, monumentally hard and deep, down Brian's throat. Nicolai did not know if he'd said anything or if he'd screamed, but as he came back to himself, his throat ached slightly, and he wondered just what he'd said in the throes of the passion that Brian had given him. Eyes closed, still breathing hard, Nicolai lay on the cushions and let the afterglow wash over him, enjoying the pleasant tingle that seemed to emanate from every part of him.

Slowly, Nicolai cracked his eyes open and saw Brian smiling from above him. Nicolai reached up and pulled him down into a deep kiss before beginning to work on the buttons of Brian's shirt. He wanted Brian's skin, needed to feel him. Once he got the shirt off, he saw Brian stand up and first pull off the rest of Nicolai's clothes before stripping down himself. Nicolai was going to ask if they should go upstairs, but then Brian was on top of him, skin to skin, and Nicolai didn't care where they made love, as long as Brian was with him.

The kisses continued, and Nicolai felt Brian moving against his skin, hard and smooth, already restoking his desire. Nicolai tapped Brian's hip and then felt him moving on the sofa, repositioning until Nicolai was on top. He wanted to make his lover feel just as wonderful as Brian had made him feel. Nicolai grinned into Brian's glistening eyes before slinking down his body, lips licking and kissing hot skin. When he reached Brian's throbbing erection, he didn't tease or preamble, he simply took him deep, sucking and licking the hard shaft.

There weren't many times that he regretted losing his hearing. He'd long gotten over the loss and learned to live with it, but right now, watching the way Brian's eyes danced and the way his mouth hung open, he knew Brian was making incredible sounds that were completely lost to him. Just once he wished he could hear what he was doing to his lover. Nicolai could feel the pleasure rippling through Brian, and he could see the way his eyes danced and the way his chest caught when Nicolai swirled his tongue beneath the large head of Brian's cock. He'd never given it a thought before, certainly not with Justin, but in this moment it was what he longed for, even if only for a moment.

Brian's hips bucked slightly, and Nicolai knew Brian was getting close. He sucked harder, taking Brian deep, encouraging his lover's pleasure. He felt Brian throb against his lips and Nicolai stilled, feeling Brian's cock jump against his lips just before he came, and Nicolai took everything he had to give, encouraging Brian to take all the pleasure he could.

Letting Brian slip from his lips, Nicolai climbed back up his body, meeting Brian's glowing eyes. Feeling Brian's hands on his cheeks, Nicolai let Brian guide him to his lips for a kiss that stole his breath away. Nicolai clung to Brian, holding him tight through the kiss and for long after. How long he remained on top of Brian's body he didn't know, but he was warm and Brian felt so comfortable. He didn't want to move because that would mean giving up the closeness that he loved so much.

Soon, regardless of what he wanted, Nicolai felt Brian shift beneath him, and he knew their time was over. Nicolai knew he shouldn't be, but he was jealous of Brian's daughter, because she would get to spend the rest of the evening with Brian, and Nicolai would be left at home, alone. It was on the tip of his tongue to ask him when he intended to explain things to Zoe, but he stopped himself. He had no right to ask him to rush something that could be so important. But he didn't want to feel like a guilty little secret, either. "I don't want to go," Nicolai saw Brian tell him. "I want to stay with you." It almost seemed like Brian was reading his mind. Then Brian bent down to kiss him.

Once the kiss broke, Nicolai lay naked on the sofa and watched as Brian got dressed. Nicolai knew Brian had to get home before his mother dropped off Zoe, but he hated seeing him leave. Brian had his pants on and was pulling on his shirt when he hurried out of the room, returning a few minutes later carrying a blanket that he spread over Nicolai, making sure he was tucked in. Then Brian kissed him one more time before pulling on the rest of his clothes. Nicolai watched as Brian pulled on his coat. Then he waved before leaving the house. Nicolai could feel the front door close. Sitting up, he watched out the window as Brian got into his car and drove away. Once he was gone, Nicolai lay back down and closed his eyes, thinking how good he felt when Brian was around and how much he missed him and wished they were together when Brian was gone.

Nicolai knew Brian telling Zoe wasn't the issue. He'd developed feelings for Brian that went beyond what he'd felt for anyone else. He had to face it—he was in love with Brian. The thing was, he wasn't sure how Brian felt about him. He knew Brian liked him, and they were good together in bed. He also knew that he had a connection with Brian and felt comfortable with him, and Brian seemed to care about his thoughts. He seemed to listen to him most of the time, but how he really felt, Nicolai just wasn't sure. Lying on the sofa, Nicolai stared at the ceiling like it was going to magically provide him the answers.

He saw the light in the hallway flash once and then twice indicating that someone was at the door. He tried looking out the window, but couldn't see who was there. Getting up, he pulled on his pants and padded toward the front door and opened it, thinking Brian had come back. Instead, he found he was staring into Justin's eyes. Nicolai stepped back and tried to close the door, but Justin stepped forward and muscled his way into the house.

"What are you doing here?" Nicolai asked, closing the door before crossing his arms in front of his bare chest.

"You wouldn't return my messages, and I was worried about you," Justin signed.

"I didn't return your texts because I don't have anything to say to you and I want you to leave me alone. It's over, and I'm not interested in getting back together. I've moved on, and it's time you did too," Nicolai signed as he looked at Justin and saw a glimpse of the heartache Justin was feeling. "I know you're hurting, but we can't go back to where we were."

"I want you back, Nicky, I really do."

Nicolai shook his head before opening the door. "I'm sorry, Justin, but you need to go," Nicolai signed, and he waited for Justin to leave. He looked as though he was going to do just that when Nicolai saw him peer into the living room and then back at him. Justin's face grew red and the resigned look on his face faded as

Justin glared at him with a look that sent a shiver up Nicolai's spine that he knew wasn't from the cold.

"You were with him! Weren't you?" Justin signed rapidly, punctuating his signs with jabs to the air.

"Justin, it's time for you to go," Nicolai signed, and he motioned toward the door. He had no intention of answering any of Justin's questions. "Just get out and stay away."

Justin glared at him once again, eyes hard, mouth set in a scowl as he stepped toward the door. He looked as though he were going to say something, but Nicolai pushed Justin out the door and slammed it closed hard enough that he could feel the reverberation through his body. Throwing the lock, Nicolai made sure all the doors were locked tight before peering out the front windows to make sure Justin's car was gone. Only then did he sit back down on the sofa and pull the blanket around him as he began to shiver.

CHAPTER 5

"DIETER, honey, it's only been a month. The courts often take their time in rendering their decisions," Brian let Gerald explain as they talked to his lover through Gerald's office speaker phone.

"This isn't unusual," Brian added, trying to calm the nervous man. "You just have to be patient a little longer. Once we hear, I promise you'll be the first to know. If it's possible, Nicolai is almost as nervous and impatient as you."

"I know. We text each other almost every day, and he's been really wonderful," Dieter said, some of his nervous impatience gone from his voice. "I'm sorry to bug."

"You aren't, honey," Gerald said soothingly. "We'll talk about it tonight when I get home." Gerald picked up the phone, and Brian ignored them while they talked in low tones. Then Gerald hung up and looked at Brian. "Is this much time really normal?"

"No. Decisions usually take a few weeks, and I'm not sure if the delay is good news or not. There are attorneys who have studied these kinds of things, and they come to one conclusion—they can't decide either." Brian ate the last bite of his sandwich before crumpling the paper and throwing it in the trash. "We need to go over the Simpson case before court next week. Is it okay if we start while you eat?" Brian asked, and to his surprise, Gerald shook his head.

"Dieter made me swear not to say anything to you, but I feel like I have to. Is there something going on with you and Nicolai? Dieter says he's been really nervous and jumpy lately, and all he'll say is that there's nothing wrong. But Dieter says there has to be because that's not like him. When Nicolai was at the house yesterday to return the painting he'd been working on, I touched his shoulder to get his attention, and he nearly dropped the painting he was holding as he jumped away."

"I've seen it, too, but he keeps insisting he's fine. At first I thought he was upset with me," Brian explained. He hadn't really wanted to talk about this with anyone other than Nicolai, but he trusted Gerald, and he really needed some advice. "I know he isn't happy that we don't get to see each other very often. Zoe loves him, but I haven't told her about us yet."

"Why?" Gerald asked after he swallowed his last bite of sandwich, placing the trash in the can near his desk. "You care for Nicolai, don't you?"

Brian thought for a few seconds, trying to put conflicting feelings into words. "Yes, I do. But I don't want Zoe disappointed. If I tell her and things don't work out, she could get hurt, and that's the last thing I want. My getting hurt is bad enough, but I can't bear hurting Zoe. She's been through a lot, and she really likes Nicolai. I know that."

"Okay," Gerald said in his lawyerly voice, and Brian wondered what was coming. "Zoe is one of the best kids I've ever met. She's smart and as loving a soul as I've ever come across. If you want my opinion, I think in this case, you need to treat her as a young lady and tell her the truth. She'll make up her own mind, like she does with just about everything else, because I can tell you if I were in her place, I'd want to know and I'd be angry if you didn't tell me." Gerald's voice was as serious as Brian had ever heard him, even in court. "Think about this as well. The last thing you want is for her to find out on her own or from someone else. She needs to hear it from you first."

"How'd you get so smart?" Brian asked softly, his insides doing flip-flops.

"By making plenty of mistakes myself. Coming out isn't easy for anyone. But I can almost guarantee that whatever you're thinking is much worse than reality. I know it was for me. Dieter and I are here for you. You know that. So think about what's best for you and Zoe, and don't worry about what anyone else is going to say or how they will react." Gerald reached into his desk and pulled out a pad and a brief. "Sorry for getting on my soapbox. You need to do what's right and forget about what anyone else thinks, including me."

Brian nodded his understanding, wondering if Gerald wasn't correct. He knew he'd have to think it over, but maybe Gerald was right. Maybe he needed to let Zoe make up her own mind. "Let's get to work."

Gerald agreed, and they spent the next hour reviewing the case and deciding on a strategy for court. Then Brian went back to his office and closed the door. Thankfully it was a Friday afternoon, and he didn't have any appointments. He needed some time to think. What Gerald said really made sense, and truthfully, he wasn't worried about Zoe's reaction so much as Barbara's when she found out. "Be a man," he told himself out loud. Keeping his door closed, Brian worked on his other cases, using the quiet time to clear his thoughts and make some headway.

A knock on the door pulled him out of the deposition he'd been reading. "Come in," Brian called, and Gerald stepped into his office.

"Will we see you and Nicolai for dinner tomorrow?" Gerald asked.

"Is it okay if I bring Zoe? She's supposed to be with her mother this weekend, but I never know."

"Of course. Zoe's always welcome. You know that. Just let us know," Gerald responded before breaking into a smile. "You know Dieter. He has to have something for her when she comes over."

"I know." Brian smiled as he closed the files he'd been working on. "He spoils her rotten. It's no wonder she'd rather come to your house than go see her mother." Brian smiled at Zoe's Uncle Gerald. "I'm about to get out of here for the weekend. You go home, too, and I'll see you tomorrow."

Brian finished packing his things and was about to leave when his phone rang. "Brian Watson."

"Mr. Watson, I'm the head clerk from the federal district court in Chicago, and I was instructed to call you."

IN THE car that evening after leaving his office, Brian pressed the answer button on his steering wheel as he drove home. "Hello."

"Brian, this is Barbara. I can't take Zoe tonight. I have to go to my mother's. She isn't feeling well, but I'll be by to pick her up first thing in the morning. Is that all right?"

To Brian's near shock, she sounded sober and, dare he think, nice.

"That's okay. I'll see you in the morning, and I hope your mother feels better." What else could he say? The call disconnected, and Brian huffed to himself as he checked the time, realizing that Nicolai had probably already left home. He decided he'd deal with it when he got to the house. Driving the rest of the way, Brian parked in the garage and hurried inside.

Zoe and Georgia were sitting on the sofa downstairs, books on both their laps. "Daddy," Zoe called as she set her book aside, grabbed a paper, and rushed to him for a hug. "My report card came today." She waved the paper in front of him, squirming with excitement.

"Well, let's see," Brian said, putting her down.

"I have to go," Georgia told him, already packing away her books. "I'll see you both on Monday." Georgia hugged Brian as well as Zoe before putting on her coat.

"If you give me a minute, I can write you a check," Brian told her, and Georgia rolled her eyes. Brian pulled out his wallet, handing her cash instead, which earned him a smile.

"See you Monday, squirt," Georgia teased, and Zoe giggled.

"Bye, pickle-warts," she retorted as Georgia closed the door. Zoe continued giggling as Brian carried her into the living room, sitting on the sofa, and Zoe settled next to him. They looked at her report card together. She got high marks in everything except spelling, but even there, she was doing well.

"You did great, and I'm really proud of you," Brian said as he bear-hugged Zoe, complete with growly noises that were met with giggles. "There's something I want to talk to you about, and it's important. It's about me and Nicolai."

"Is Nicolai your boyfriend?" Zoe asked, her giggles fading away, eyes wide and serious.

Brian's eyes widened in surprise at his daughter's perception, and he swallowed before answering, "Yes, he is."

"Okay. Janey has two mommies, and she says it's cool." Zoe slipped off the sofa, walking toward the stairs. "Is Mommy coming?"

"She called. She's going to pick you up in the morning," Brian answered as he motioned for Zoe to come back. "How did you know?"

Zoe put her hands on her hips and rolled her eyes in a big circle. "I'm not dumb, Daddy," she answered like he'd just asked the most stupid question in the world.

"No, you're not," Brian said as he reached for her, tickling her until they were both squirming and laughing. "You're a very smart girl, and I'm so proud of you, and I love you so much," Brian told her with a huge smile on his face. "Nicolai is going to come for dinner. Is that okay?"

"Is he gonna cook? 'Cause your food is yucky." She made a face that left no doubt whatsoever what she thought of his cooking.

"If you ask him nicely with your hands, I bet he'll help."

The doorbell rang, and Zoe hurried to answer it. Brian felt the cool breeze from the door opening and then quiet. Peering out, he saw Zoe and Nicolai signing their hellos, with Nicolai grinning at the young girl.

"She's been practicing," Nicolai told him when he walked into the living room with Zoe right behind him.

"We both have," Brian signed before adding, "but we could use more practice." Brian spelled out the words he didn't know, but it was getting easier for him. "The classes are fun, and we have a good teacher."

Brian turned to Zoe. "Take your books upstairs and get ready for dinner. You can help in the kitchen." Zoe grabbed her books off the sofa and raced out of the room and up the stairs. "I told her about us this evening," Brian told Nicolai. "She asked me if you were my boyfriend, and I told her you were."

"So it was no problem?" Nicolai asked, and Brian nodded his yes.

Zoe bounded down the stairs and into Nicolai's legs. "Are you going to have a sleepover with Daddy like Mommy does with Jeff?"

"Who's Jeff?" Brian quizzed.

"Mommy's boyfriend," Zoe answered. "He's a lawyer like you."

"Let's get dinner started," Brian suggested with enthusiasm, hoping to pull the conversation away from his love life and onto something he was more comfortable talking about. Zoe hurried into the kitchen, and Brian caught Nicolai's attention, glad to see him smile. "Will you help with dinner?"

"I'd better," Nicolai signed. "Remember, I've tasted your cooking too," he added with a grin, and Brian tried to look offended, but just couldn't manage it.

"Then you better rescue all of us from my cooking," Brian retorted as he motioned toward the kitchen.

Zoe insisted on chicken nuggets, so Nicolai put some in the oven for her before broiling steaks for the two of them. Brian made the salad and set the table while Nicolai finished dinner. He found it really nice—he liked doing things with Nicolai, even if it was kitchen things. Once dinner was ready, they carried the food into the dining room, Brian poured the wine, and the three of them sat down to eat.

Conversation was light, and Brian saw Nicolai looking alternately at him and Zoe as they talked. This felt right—easy and compatible in a way things never had with Barbara, no matter how hard he'd tried.

"After dinner will you play video games with me?" Zoe asked Nicolai, who nodded and smiled his answer. Brian knew Nicolai couldn't hear Zoe's cry of excitement, thank goodness. Brian loved his daughter dearly, but those high-pitched screams would cut through concrete.

"Calm down and eat. We'll play video games after you've finished your dinner," Brian coaxed his daughter, and she sat back down on her chair and began to eat once again, taking a few bites before chattering away again. Brian ate and watched Nicolai, reading a bit of confusion and nervousness in his posture. Reaching under the table, Brian patted Nicolai's leg to reassure him, and earned a slight smile. "We will talk after Zoe goes to bed," Brian mouthed when Zoe hurried to the kitchen to get a juice box.

"Okay," Nicolai answered.

Zoe returned to the table, climbing back onto her chair and continuing to chatter away about school and what the other kids said and did. Brian paid attention to about half of it, the rest of his mind on Nicolai. He'd missed him, a lot. Brian's life was full with work and Zoe, but it didn't feel quite complete unless he was with Nicolai, and he sighed contentedly as he watched Zoe ask Nicolai the signs for everything on the table. He loved how patient Nicolai was as he showed Zoe the signs for everything from knife and salt shaker to candle holder, correcting her gently when she needed it.

"Are you done?" Brian asked when it became evident that Zoe wasn't going to eat another bite. "Because there isn't going to be food in an hour, and no before-bed snacks unless you finish your dinner," Brian chastised lightly. Zoe grabbed the last chicken nugget off her plate, eating it quickly before grinning mischievously at him. "Put your plate in the kitchen, and make sure your homework is done. When we're done eating, we'll go upstairs for a while."

"All right, Daddy," Zoe replied with a roll of her eyes, but she picked up her plate, anyway, and Brian heard the clink as she placed it on the counter and then he heard her rummaging for her books. Brian returned to his dinner, his full attention on his lover and friend.

"I have something to tell you, and you are not going to like it," Nicolai said, and Brian set down his fork, waiting for Nicolai to continue. "I thought I could handle it, but now I'm not so sure. Justin has been texting me almost every day for months. Mostly I just delete them."

Brian felt his blood pressure begin to rise as the anger boiled up from deep in his gut. His first thought was why hadn't Nicolai told him earlier, but he told himself he couldn't be angry or upset with Nicolai. This wasn't his fault. Brian took a deep breath and released it. "Tell me from the start," Brian signed, or at least close enough that Nicolai understood.

"After we got back from Chicago, and you left after…." Nicolai looked toward the other room, and Brian nodded, remembering that evening vividly. "Justin showed up, and I tried to talk to him. Eventually, I threw him out of the house. He hasn't been by the house again, but he keeps sending text messages, and sometimes I think I see him following me. I can't be sure, but I just know he's there. I thought I felt him watching me when I left my house to come here, but I haven't seen any sign of him."

"Do you know what he wants? Why he's after you?" Brian asked, keeping his frustration and the urge to find and kill the other man under control.

"No. I wish I did. For some reason, he wants me and says he loves me. But he left me and now he's got some obsession with me. I just want him to leave me alone."

"Do you still have his text messages? We could get a restraining order if we had some proof."

"I deleted all of them. I didn't want anything to do with him."

"Would you keep them in the future?" Brian asked. "We may need them." Nicolai nodded reluctantly. "Do you remember when we got home and you said something didn't feel right in your house? Do you think that could have been him? Do you think he's been inside your house?" Brian hated asking these questions, especially after he saw Nicolai's face and the fear that flashed in his eyes.

"I don't think so. That day, it was just a feeling, and nothing has been moved or taken."

"I know. But I trust your feelings. Tomorrow we're going to go to your house and check things over. If he has been in the house, then he was there for a reason of some kind," Brian said, but he didn't want to elaborate. He was more afraid that something might have been left in the house, but Brian kept that to himself for now. "Has he confronted you again?"

"No. I haven't actually spoken to him in almost a month."

"Is that why you've been so nervous and jumpy? Gerald mentioned that he was concerned about you." Brian hoped he wasn't betraying a confidence, but he was worried.

"Yes. I keep looking for Justin everywhere and expecting to turn around and see him all the time," Nicolai explained, his voice faltering slightly.

Brian got up and walked to where Nicolai was playing with the food on his plate, watching as Nicolai's gaze followed him. "It's okay. I'm here, and we'll figure out what to do. I promise." Brian slid his arms around Nicolai's waist, nuzzling the side of Nicolai's head.

"Ooooh," he heard from the other room, "kisssssiiing." Brian stopped himself from laughing at his daughter's reaction to seeing him being affectionate.

"Zoe, finish your homework," Brian said, and he heard her giggle in the other room. Brian nuzzled Nicolai one more time before returning to his chair, realizing just how careful he needed to be around Zoe. Her knowing about them was one thing, but seeing them hugging or kissing was something else. He wasn't sure it was a bad thing; he just needed to think about it.

Staring down at his plate, Brian found his appetite had gone. The food was amazing, but he didn't want to eat it. His stomach turned over a few times at the thought of anyone threatening Nicolai, his Nicolai. Brian knew he could be a bit possessive, but he wasn't jealous, he knew that—he was protective. Yes, that was the word that flashed through his mind: protective. Looking to Nicolai, he noticed that he wasn't eating, either. "Are you finished?" Brian asked when Nicolai looked at him, and he nodded.

"I didn't mean to ruin dinner," Nicolai said as he signed.

"Justin did," Brian signed as best he could before getting up and carrying the plates into the kitchen.

Zoe looked up from her papers. "Can we go play games now?"

"Go ask Nicolai nicely if he wants to, and I'll be up as soon as I finish with the dishes." Everything felt so domestic, so contentedly settled. He knew it was an illusion, at least for now, but it was a happy one, and he didn't want to do anything to shatter it, no matter how inevitable that was.

Brian took care of the dishes before cleaning up the kitchen and turning off the lights. Walking up the stairs, he heard Zoe's excited laughter and the sounds of speeding cars, skids, and the occasional crash. He also heard Nicolai's unabashed laughter, which, the few times he'd heard it, sounded pure and nearly childlike. Brian figured that since he couldn't hear himself, he never learned to censor or alter his laughter. To Brian's ears, the mixture of the two happy sounds was like fine music. Stepping into the room, Brian waited until their game was over, and then Zoe handed him her controller, indicating that she wanted her father and Nicolai to race. She started the game and then sat back on the sofa, calling out encouragement to both of them at the top of her lungs.

Nicolai easily kicked his ass all over the track, and when the game was over, he handed Zoe back her controller and sat back to let the two of them duel it out. The next race was surprisingly close, but Nicolai got some kind of bullet power boost at the end and flew by Zoe to cross the line first. To her credit, Zoe jumped up and down with as much excitement for Nicolai as if she'd won.

"Okay, one more game, and then it's time for bed," Brian said, and Zoe stopped jumping, a look of disgust on her face.

"It's Friday night, Dad," she said, accentuated with her patented eye roll.

"Your mother will be here in the morning, and if you aren't out of bed and ready when she gets here...." Brian began, and he saw some of the air go out of Zoe's proverbial balloon.

"She'll scream like a dog from h-e-double toothpicks," Zoe finished.

"Exactly, so play another game and then get ready for bed. You can read before you turn out your light." That seemed to mollify her, and Brian watched as she restarted the game once again. This time she won and collected high fives from both of them before putting the game away and cleaning up her toys. "Get cleaned up and I'll tuck you in," Brian told her, and she left the room, footsteps fading down the hall.

"I should go home," Nicolai said before getting to his feet.

"No. Please don't," Brian said before realizing Nicolai couldn't have known he'd said anything. Touching Nicolai's arm, Brian caught his eye as Nicolai turned. "Please stay."

Nicolai looked toward the door to the hallway where Zoe had raced out, before turning back to him.

"I want you to stay," Brian said softly. What he really wanted was for Nicolai to stay with him in his bed, but he didn't think he should risk that with Zoe in the house, but that didn't stop him from wanting, or his body from remembering what it felt like to have Nicolai's skin close to him. A small shiver ran up his body at the thought. Nicolai's small nod and the warm look in his eyes told Brian that Nicolai felt the same way.

"I'm ready, Daddy," Zoe called, and after explaining things to Nicolai, Brian got up to make sure Zoe was ready for bed.

Half an hour later, Brian walked downstairs through the dark, quiet house. Zoe had turned off her light, and after a minimum of fuss was already asleep. Brian found Nicolai in the living room, sitting on the sofa, reading a book. He looked so peaceful and.... Brian did a double take before touching Nicolai's arm. "I didn't know you wore glasses," Brian mouthed, wishing he knew the signs.

"Sometimes my eyes get tired," Nicolai explained before setting his book aside and reaching to pull off the glasses, collapsing them into a surprisingly tiny case that he'd seen but never paid attention to.

Brian shook his head, moving in for a kiss. "They are sexy," Brian said, and tried to sign, but ended up spelling the last word. But it had the desired effect, and Nicolai blushed as Brian touched his lips, feeling Nicolai respond. Brian knew they shouldn't do more than kiss, but he wanted Nicolai so badly he could feel his need overwhelming his judgment, and he forced himself to back away. "Do you want to read some more?"

Nicolai shook his head before turning off the lamp and following him upstairs. Brian went to his room and used the master bath to clean up before getting ready for bed. As he climbed into bed, he heard Nicolai moving through the house. Brian reached to turn out the light and saw his door open, Nicolai stepping inside. He'd meant for him to use the guest room, but watching as his robe fell to the floor was too much, and he lifted the bedding so Nicolai could join him.

Brian sighed when he felt Nicolai curl right next to him, where he felt perfect. Brian loved how they fit together, and the way Nicolai always seemed cold and wanted to get as close as possible. Brian stroked his hand along Nicolai's cheek, and then suddenly, Nicolai had shifted on top of him, beautiful eyes shining down at him. And then Nicolai was kissing him, hard. Brian kissed back just as hard, hands caressing down Nicolai's back, and as he reached the curve of Nicolai's back, he felt Nicolai quiver against him.

Brian felt Nicolai's sizable excitement sliding along his hip. Brian's body had already reacted with gusto, and he hugged Nicolai tight, tasting his lips as his hands wandered over warm, sensual skin.

A soft sound drifted into the room, and Brian stilled. Nicolai lifted his head, and Brian mouthed, "Zoe" as he continued to listen. Brian heard nothing more and felt Nicolai's warmth slip away as he slid onto the sheets. To Brian's surprise, Nicolai lifted the covers and got out of the bed, picking his robe off the floor and sliding it onto his shoulders. Brian knew Nicolai was going to the guest room, and he thought that was probably for the best. If Barbara arrived early in the morning and somehow caught them, there would be screaming hell to pay.

Brian watched as Nicolai closed and tied his robe. *What am I doing?* Brian asked himself. *I'm letting my ex-wife determine the relationship I have with someone I care for.* As Nicolai reached the door, Brian threw back the covers and walked to Nicolai, touching him lightly on the shoulder. When Nicolai turned around, Brian took his hand and gently led him back to the bed. Opening Nicolai's robe, Brian slipped it off his shoulders and let it pool on the floor before guiding him into the bed. They probably shouldn't make love, but he'd be damned if he was going to let Nicolai sleep in the guest room of his home. Brian pulled the covers over both of them, holding Nicolai tight. He still wished they could make love, but being close to Nicolai was indescribably better than having him sleep in the guest room. Saying good night with a soft kiss, Brian rolled onto his side, spooning to Nicolai's back as he tried to fall asleep.

Brian had found out very quickly that Nicolai in his bed meant he was too excited to really sleep. For most of the night, Brian dozed on and off, but he was always keenly aware of the warm, beautifully sexy man in his bed. The first light had begun filtering through the windows when Brian finally drifted into a deep sleep. He felt Nicolai move next to him, and he tightened his grip; it was too early for them to get out of bed. Brian might have said something, he wasn't sure, but he kept his eyes closed even when Nicolai left the bed. It wasn't until he realized that Nicolai wasn't returning that Brian finally opened his eyes. He heard movement downstairs, and Brian got out of bed, pulling on a pair of sweatpants and a T-shirt before padding down the stairs, barely paying attention to where he was going until he nearly tripped on the last step.

"I made breakfast, Daddy!" Zoe cried as he reached the kitchen, and Brian was instantly awake. He nearly gasped at the mess and the pile of toast with jam that she'd put on a plate. Zoe carried the plate to the table, a huge smile on her face. Brian grabbed a rag and began wiping up the jam and butter that were spread all over the counter. Looking up, he saw Nicolai wander in from the bathroom, already dressed, with an amused look on his face.

"Come in and eat," Zoe said, taking Nicolai's hand before practically dragging him into the dining room. Brian followed and saw that plates had been set out, along with knives, forks, and glasses. A huge plate of toast sat in the center of the table with a carton of orange juice and nothing else. Nicolai looked at him, and Brian winked back and shrugged, with Nicolai smiling back. Zoe picked up the carton of juice.

"I'll pour, okay?" Brian took the carton from her and poured them each a glass of juice. Then he made the mistake of trying to take a piece of toast, and the whole stack moved as one on the plate. Zoe had spread jam on the bread and then stacked the pieces on top of each other, sticking them all together. Brian managed to get a piece off the stack and gingerly placed it onto Nicolai's plate before getting one of his own. They ate their toast with a knife and fork, with Brian looking down at his plate to keep Zoe from seeing his near laughter.

The doorbell rang, and Brian breathed a sigh of relief. Zoe raced off to answer it, and she returned with Barbara right behind her. "Isn't she ready yet?" Barbara asked impatiently.

"Zoe made breakfast," Brian explained calmly. "Zoe, get your mother a plate."

Barbara looked over the table and shook her head, looking curiously at Nicolai. "Honey, we need to go. Are you packed?" Her snide tone was gone.

"Yes," Zoe answered, and she took a last bite of her toast before rushing away.

"Be sure to wash your hands," Brian called as Zoe raced upstairs.

"Who are you and what are you doing here this early in the morning?" Barbara snapped at Nicolai as soon as Zoe was out of earshot. He was valiantly trying to finish his toast, but the last piece appeared stuck to his plate, and he was concentrating on that and not looking at her.

"This is Nicolai," Brian explained. "You need to look at him when you speak, so he can read your lips." That seemed to take some of the wind out of Barbara's sails, at least on that subject.

"You left her alone in the kitchen?" Barbara commented, finding something else to criticize.

"She made toast. Zoe's growing up, and she needs to do things on her own. Granted, this didn't turn out very well, but she's learning, and she has to do that." Brian finished his juice before pushing back his chair as he heard Zoe coming down the stairs, and he lightly touched Nicolai's arm before getting up from the table.

Brian helped Zoe with her small suitcase before saying good-bye to his daughter and giving her a big hug and a kiss. "What time do you expect to have her back tomorrow?" Brian asked Barbara, who turned her attention away from the table and Nicolai.

"I'll bring her back after dinner," Barbara answered.

"Did you pack your homework?" Brian asked, and Zoe shook her head.

"I did it already," Zoe answered before grabbing her suitcase and hurrying outside. Barbara followed without saying anything, and Brian closed the door, breathing an inward sigh of relief.

"I think you deserve to be taken out for a proper breakfast," Brian said to Nicolai, who simply smiled as he stepped closer, a wickedly sinful look on his face. Brian needed no words to tell him what that look meant. Nicolai walked right up to him, pressing Brian back against the door before kissing him with pent-up desire.

"You are breakfast," Nicolai sort of growled before kissing him hard once again. Brian loved this aggressive side to Nicolai and relished the feeling of Nicolai's body pressed to his, his arousal making itself known. Brian waited to see what Nicolai would do next. He didn't have long to wait. The hem of his T-shirt was grabbed, and Nicolai hauled the shirt over his head before throwing it in a corner. Brian's head banged back against the door, and he barely felt it as his nipples were sucked. Nicolai then licked down his stomach, and before he could think, Brian's sweatpants were around his ankles, and Nicolai took him deep in a single breath-stealing movement.

Brian kept his head against the door and thought he was going to scream. Hell, he did scream. It didn't matter if Nicolai couldn't hear it—he couldn't have stopped it if he tried. Stroking Nicolai's hair, Brian tried not to thrust into Nicolai's hot mouth, but he couldn't stop that, either. Spending the entire night next to Nicolai and not being able to do anything about it had kept Brian on a knife edge for hours, and he was about to embarrass himself completely because Brian could already feel the tingling at the base of his spine and he was already gasping for breath. Trying to control himself bought him a few seconds, and then he was coming, hard, eyes clamped closed as he tried not to collapse onto the floor.

Thank God the door was there, because it was the only thing keeping Brian upright. It felt as though Nicolai had sucked his spine and brain out of him. Opening his eyes, Brian steadied himself as Nicolai stood back up, kissing Brian again, his lover's body vibrating with desire, eyes wide and wanting. It took Brian a few minutes to catch his breath, and once he did, he engulfed Nicolai into a bear hug before twirling them around until it was Nicolai pressed back against the door. Without preamble, Brian worked open Nicolai's pants, yanking them down his legs. Brian took a few seconds to admire the view as he sank to his knees: long, thick cock, standing tall, heavy balls, aching for release. Brian stroked Nicolai's length and heard those involuntary sounds. They increased in intensity as he ran his tongue from base to tip. Nicolai hadn't teased, and Brian wasn't about to either. Taking a cue from Nicolai, Brian opened his mouth and took Nicolai as deep and hard as he could.

Nicolai made a noise unlike anything Brian had heard from him before, and he felt Nicolai's legs shake as he bobbed his head and sucked. Brian loved the way Nicolai's cock felt as it slid over his tongue. In the past few months, Brian had discovered that not only did he enjoy sucking cock, but Nicolai drove him crazy—the taste, the scent, it all flipped his switch, and from the sounds Nicolai was making, what he was doing was certainly turning Nicolai's crank. Brian ran his hand up Nicolai's bare legs to cup his butt, placing a finger at Nicolai's opening, pressing lightly as he sucked harder. He felt Nicolai's breath catch and his muscles tighten. Brian knew Nicolai was close, and he worked a little harder, pulling Nicolai over the edge.

Brian swallowed everything Nicolai had to offer before slowly letting him slip from his lips. Standing up, he kissed Nicolai hard, his lover breathing like he'd just run a marathon. Brian felt Nicolai's arms around his neck, and they kissed for a long time until he felt Nicolai begin to shiver slightly.

After getting dressed, they spent the day with each other. They really didn't do much other than spend time together. At one point, they read on the sofa with Nicolai's legs stretched over Brian's. "We should get ready for dinner," Brian signed to Nicolai as best he could before Nicolai gently corrected him.

"Yes. Dieter will worry if we're late," Nicolai said, but he made no move to lower his legs. Brian was pretty comfortable himself, and only dinner with their close friends would have gotten them to move. Reluctantly, they disentangled themselves from each other and got ready to leave.

"I want to stop by your house on our way, just to make sure everything is okay," Brian told Nicolai before they got in the car.

"Do you really think Justin could have done something in my house?" Nicolai asked, and Brian saw the nervousness in his eyes and wished he hadn't brought the subject up again.

"I don't know," Brian told Nicolai, "but I want you to be safe." Brian touched Nicolai's leg, squeezing lightly before starting the car and pulling out of the garage.

The drive to Nicolai's didn't take long, and they both went inside. "Does everything seem okay?" Brian asked, and Nicolai nodded slowly before wandering through the house. Brian wasn't sure what he was looking for, but kept his eyes open. Neither of them saw anything out of the ordinary, so they left, locking the door behind them before heading to Gerald and Dieter's.

The front door opened as soon as they drove up, with Dieter grinning at them as they got out of the car. Brian grabbed a bag from the backseat and walked toward the front door. Going inside, they were both hugged before Dieter pulled Nicolai away, the two of them talking with their hands and expressions.

"I swear those two are like brothers," Gerald said from behind him, and Brian turned, hugging his friend and colleague. "I think Dieter always wanted a brother, and he seems to have adopted Nicolai," Gerald said, his eyes shining at Dieter. "What's this?" he asked when he noticed the bag. Brian handed it to him, and Gerald pulled out the champagne. "Let me get some glasses."

Gerald popped open the bottle and poured four glasses before handing one to each of them. "To good friends," Gerald said before raising his glass. They all sipped, and then Brian cleared his throat before looking at Nicolai so he could follow along.

"I received a call from the district court clerk." Brian tried to keep the grin off his face. "The panel's opinion has yet to be filed, but they affirmed the lower court's decision. We won."

Nicolai handed Brian his glass and hugged Dieter, the two of them jumping and bouncing like little children, while Gerald lifted his glass, taking Dieter's to keep it from spilling. Both he and Gerald watched their lovers celebrate for a few seconds, then Gerald raised his glass, and Brian did the same before taking a sip. "Guys," Brian said. First Dieter and then Nicolai stopped their bouncing. "I hate to throw a wet blanket on this party, but this is only the next step."

"But we won," Dieter said with a huge smile still on his face.

"Yes, we did, and this is good news. But this case isn't over yet. There's a lot that can happen. The case will certainly be appealed again, and it's also possible that this scared them enough that the Austrians will propose some sort of settlement. Now, if they appeal, that doesn't mean the Supreme Court will take the case, and if they decline to take it, then the rulings in our favor stand. But this could be dragged out for quite some time yet."

"But we still won," Dieter insisted, and he went back to his bouncing, hugging first Nicolai and then Gerald, and soon Brian found himself caught up in the excitement. They had won, something most lawyers wouldn't have expected. Brian himself had had his doubts, but as he looked at Nicolai, he remembered what he'd said about the judges' expressions and reactions at the hearing. Nicolai had been spot-on. He'd said the judges seemed to be reacting in their favor, and Brian had discounted it.

Nicolai and Dieter broke apart, with Dieter hugging Gerald for all he was worth. It was good to see him happy. Placing an arm around Nicolai's waist, Brian tugged him close and handed Nicolai back his glass. Brian remembered the shy, quiet man Dieter had been when he'd first come to the law firm carrying his grandmother's photo albums. He'd looked so small then, but now, he was so full of life and confidence. It was gratifying to see, and a bit of an inspiration.

"Why don't we move into the living room? Dieter and I have a bit more news to share, and something we'd like to ask the two of you," Gerald said with a gesture toward the large, comfortable room, where they sat down, with Nicolai next to Brian on the sofa. Once they were comfortable, Gerald nudged Dieter lightly.

"I believe Gerald talked to you, Brian, about this a while ago, but we're going to Vienna in June and wondered if both of you would like to go with us—Zoe too. You've been working so hard to help get my family heritage back, and we thought that maybe you'd like to see what you've been fighting for."

Brian looked at Nicolai and smiled. God, he'd love nothing more than to have a whole week with his lover instead of just the stolen days and hours they'd been having. Nicolai deserved more than that.

Dieter's voice pulled Brian out of his thoughts. "Since we've been sharing good news, Gerald and I have located another pair of my great-grandparents' paintings. They're in a small museum in Potsdam outside Berlin. The Germans have a very well-established process for returning looted art, and the proof we'd already gathered from the original court case was enough to get them returned. They're actually being shipped in the next few weeks." Dieter was so excited, and Brian looked at Nicolai, who seemed almost as thrilled as Dieter.

"There's one other thing," Gerald interjected. "We've also found three woodcut prints that were part of the collection. They were in a small municipal collection in Hamburg, and they arrived last night." Gerald looked at his partner, who smiled. "Dieter has decided that he wants each of you to have one of them. You've both done so much for us, and we wanted to say thank you."

Dieter stood up and left the room, returning with two small parcels wrapped in brown paper. Brian took the one Dieter offered to him, swallowing hard as he slowly opened the package. Inside was a rigid folder. When Brian opened it, he saw a small, detailed print on paper. "All three of the etchings are by Dürer," Dieter explained, and Brian knew just enough to know they were important, but it was Nicolai who gasped, and when Brian looked, he saw tears running down his lover's cheeks.

"This is too much," Nicolai said and moved to hand the package back, but Dieter shook his head. Nicolai took the package back and opened it gingerly, his face lighting when he saw the small work. Gently rewrapping the package, Nicolai handed his to Brian before standing up and scooping Dieter into a deep hug, the tears still streaming down his face. Once Nicolai let go, it was Brian's turn, and he hugged both Dieter and Gerald, thanking them in a completely inadequate way.

"The two we gave you are each one of a pair," Dieter told them, and the significance wasn't lost on Brian.

Nicolai sniffed as he sat back on the sofa, holding his package like it was the most precious gift he'd ever received. "I guess it's my turn for news. I got the commission at the Art Institute in Chicago to do the assessment of the Chagall windows. They also said in their messages that if any repairs are needed, they would discuss having me do them once the assessment is complete."

Nicolai's announcement took Brian by surprise, and he smiled, happy that Nicolai had gotten the assignment. "Will you be spending a lot of time in Chicago?" he asked. Brian knew his initial reaction was a selfish one, but he couldn't help it. He and Nicolai had so little time together, and now he was going to be in Chicago.

"The assessment will take a month or so. I'll work at the Institute three days a week. The rest of the work will be data analysis, which I can do from home. So I shouldn't be gone too much, and I expect to be home on the weekends," Nicolai explained, signing as he spoke.

Brian felt terrible. Was he so selfish that he'd feel bad or jealous that Nicolai was going to be away for a while? This was a great opportunity for him, and a huge honor. He should be happy instead of being thoughtless. Brian knew that, but he *was* feeling selfish right now, especially where Nicolai was concerned.

"Gerald and I are going to finish dinner. We shouldn't be gone for very long," Dieter said, getting up from his chair as Gerald followed.

"That was very nice of them," Brian said, indicating the drawings.

"It's too much," Nicolai insisted, still clutching his package like it was a precious object. "These are some of the finest examples of woodcut printing ever done. Dürer was a master, and these are masterpieces. Museums would fight over these engravings, and they just gave them to us," Nicolai told him, his voice becoming harder to understand because of the emotion.

Brian hadn't realized the significance of the gift he'd been given and began to wonder himself if he should return the artwork, but he knew Dieter and Gerald would be insulted, and he also knew his friends were well aware of the value of the gift. "Think of it this way. Even if these had no value, they once belonged to Dieter's family. I think that's the more important thing. Dieter wants us to be part of his family. I know he thinks of you almost like a brother." Brian gave up on trying to sign, and instead made sure he spoke clearly and as slowly as he could. Nicolai didn't look totally convinced, but when Dieter came back into the room, Nicolai stood up and hugged him again in a silent and very poignant thank-you.

Dinner was very delicious, and they spent the evening comfortably together. Brian thought that usually when friends got together, the room filled with talking, but at this get-together, there was more pointing, hand gestures, and just plain body language than there was actual conversation, and it felt right. Brian did his best to sign what little he could, but gave up. Nicolai seemed to know what was being communicated, and Brian just let things flow. As the evening wore on, they said good night and both of them thanked Dieter again for the amazing gifts before heading back to the car.

As had become their custom, the drive home was quiet, but as soon as they were inside and upstairs, they said amazing things to each other with their hands, lips, tongues, and bodies, all without actually uttering a word. They fell asleep curled together under the covers almost like puppies, with neither of them able to get enough of the other.

Brian woke to what sounded like pounding on his front door followed by an insistent ringing of the doorbell. Carefully getting out of bed, he was pleased Nicolai could hear none of the commotion as he made his way down the stairs.

At the base of the stairs, Brian looked toward the door and saw Barbara staring daggers through the window. Wondering what was going on, Brian unlocked the door, and Barbara bulldozed into the house like a tornado, with Zoe trailing behind her. Brian ignored his ex-wife to concentrate on the unhappy expression on his daughter's face.

"What's wrong, honey?"

Zoe shrugged her shoulders, and Brian lifted her into his arms before turning to glare at Barbara for an explanation. "You said you were going to keep her until after dinner. She's been looking forward to seeing you all week." Brian turned to Zoe, giving her a hug. "Go put your things up in your room and you can watch television while I talk to your mother." Brian kept his voice calm as he soothed her before putting her down.

"Is Nicolai still here?" Zoe asked, and Brian saw Barbara's eyes widen.

"Yes. He'll be up soon." Brian could feel his stomach jump, but then figured to hell with it. Barbara was not going to hold his personal life hostage, and Nicolai deserved to be acknowledged, even to his harpy of an ex-wife. Zoe hurried up the stairs, and Brian turned to Barbara. "Let's go into the living room, and you can tell me why you're here."

Brian sat down in one of the chairs and waited for her explanation.

"Is Nicolai the man who was here yesterday? What's he still doing here?" she demanded.

"You don't get to ask questions in this house. Now why are you here?" Brian pressed, knowing he'd have to answer her question eventually, but he wanted to keep control of the situation. "Let me guess, you're ditching your daughter for some guy. Am I right?"

Barbara didn't answer, and Brian knew he'd hit the nail on the head. "Well, that's just fine." Brian stood back up. "You know where the door is. Use it."

"I want an answer to my question first," Barbara demanded, her voice getting louder. Brian sat across from her, trying to tone the situation down.

"Okay. Do you remember how happy we were right after Zoe was born? We used to smile a lot and did things together. We spent time together just to be together." Barbara nodded suspiciously. "Well, I've found that again with Nicolai." Brian waited for the message to sink in.

"You're gay?" Barbara asked.

"Yes," Brian answered, and he waited to see her reaction.

Barbara's eyes widened at first, and then her face contorted into the meanest expression he'd ever seen.

"I know what you're thinking, and you can forget it. My sexual orientation has no bearing on our settlement whatsoever. I was faithful throughout our entire marriage—you weren't. I spend time with our daughter and take care of her. You toss her aside at the first opportunity. Those are the kind of facts that the courts look at. Besides, there are antidiscrimination laws in this state." Brian kept his voice calm even as he felt as though his last nerve was about to explode. He had thought telling his mother was difficult, but compared to this, his mother had been a piece of cake.

"Well, I don't want my daughter in the same house as a bunch of perverts," Barbara responded, and Brian actually began to laugh.

"Look who's talking. When was the last time you had one of your sleepovers?" Brian had to get control of the situation once again, and that seemed to do the trick. "Remember who you're talking to here. I know you almost as well as you know yourself. So think for a few minutes." Brian needed to get her calm. "When was the last time you were really happy?" Brian asked, his voice low and reassuring. "This isn't some trick. Think back to the last time you were really happy."

Barbara shook her head. "It's been so long," she answered.

"Yes, it has. We were together for a long time, but we didn't make each other happy. We were just together." Brian paused for a few seconds. "You deserve to be happy, and so do I. You need to find what will make you happy."

"Brian."

He turned and saw Nicolai standing in the doorway in his robe and bare feet, looking a bit shocked that there was someone else in the house. Nicolai turned around, and Brian hurried to him. "I'll be right up. Please don't go anywhere."

Nicolai nodded before climbing the stairs, and Brian returned to the living room. "Like I said, find what makes you happy, because I think I have." Brian didn't feel like talking anymore. The look on Nicolai's face had really gotten to Brian, and he needed to explain what was going on. "I'm sorry if you're hurt, and if you want to talk about this a little more, we can do that later, but I need to get Zoe some breakfast." Brian stepped into the hallway, and Barbara followed, looking a bit shell-shocked. And Brian had to admit, he understood how she felt. Opening the door, he held it for Barbara, who stepped outside and then turned around to look at him. "Was I that bad a wife?"

"What?" Brian asked, wondering what she meant.

"Was I such a bad wife that you turned gay?" Barbara asked, and Brian nearly laughed, but he saw she was serious.

"No. I was always gay, but you were pregnant, and we did what was right for our daughter, even if it wasn't the right thing for us," Brian explained, and Barbara nodded slowly as she walked toward her car. Brian closed the door and headed right upstairs, finding Zoe in the media room sitting on the sofa, looking rather morose.

"Daddy, did I do something to Mommy?" Zoe asked, looking about two seconds from crying.

"No, you didn't, not at all," Brian reassured her, and he held out his arms. Zoe slid off the sofa and hurried into his embrace. "Whatever happened was not your fault, and I'm glad you're back because I missed you." Brian hugged her really tight before lifting her off the ground, spinning in circles until she began to laugh.

"Daddy, I'm gonna woof," she said through peals of laughter, and he flew her to the sofa.

"We're going to go out for breakfast, so put your clothes away, and I'll come get you after I talk to Nicolai. Okay?" She hurried to her room, and Brian walked down the hall, finding Nicolai in his room, sitting on the edge of the bed.

"I did not mean to cause trouble for you," Nicolai said so softly that Brian could barely hear him.

"You didn't," Brian signed before adding, "I told her."

"But she will cause trouble for you," Nicolai countered.

"She may," Brian said as he sat next to Nicolai on the edge of the bed. "Or at least she can try. But I would rather have the truth be known than have you feel like a dirty little secret. You are more important than that. Much more important than that," Brian added for emphasis before realizing that Nicolai might not understand it. "You are important to me, and if Barbara wants to make trouble, I'll deal with it. Any trouble she makes is a small price to pay to have you in my life."

"But the trouble she makes affects Zoe," Nicolai said as he signed, his concern for Zoe touching Brian's heart. "I don't want her to be hurt."

"I know. But Barbara's already doing that, and I know you would never hurt either of us on purpose." Brian leaned closer to Nicolai, kissing him softly. "I just wish we'd had more time alone this morning."

"Daddy! I'm hungry."

"Someone's stomach is calling," he told Nicolai. "Let's get dressed, and I'll take you and Zoe to breakfast." Nicolai nodded and smiled slightly before starting to get dressed. Brian found Zoe still in the media room watching cartoons on television. "We're going to get waffles for breakfast, so get ready, and we can go as soon as I finish getting dressed."

Zoe slid off the sofa and turned on the video game. "Is Nicolai going with us?" she asked.

"Is that okay?"

"Yes. I want to show him all the new signs I've learned." She slid a disk into the game console and stopped. "Daddy, can I bring Nicolai in for show and tell?"

"Why don't you ask him at breakfast," Brian answered before returning to his room.

Nicolai stepped out of the bathroom as Brian entered the room. He looked positively edible in nothing but his pants. Sliding his arms around Nicolai's waist, Brian leaned against his back, kissing the skin behind Nicolai's ear. He wanted to drag the man back to bed, but now wasn't the time, so after one more kiss, Brian went into the bathroom to clean up. When he came out again, the room was empty. Brian dressed and left the room. He found Nicolai and Zoe in the media room, continuing their ongoing car race. Watching his daughter and boyfriend together, Brian felt his heart jump. He loved that the two most important people in the world to him got along. *It's wonderful when the people you love get along.* Brian stilled as the thought popped into his head. He loved Nicolai, and it felt right and wonderful. Brian was still nervous about actually saying the words, but he knew in his heart what he felt and it warmed him, especially when Zoe and Nicolai's game ended with Nicolai the winner, and Zoe threw herself into his arms to give him a hug.

*C*HAPTER 6

NICOLAI got out of his car and walked to his front door, sending Brian a text that he'd made it home safely.

How did it go? Brian responded with a text message.

All done, Nicolai sent with a smile. He'd spent much of the past two months traveling back and forth to Chicago, working on the Chagall windows, which, as it turned out, were in amazing condition and only needed minor repairs, which the Art Institute had him complete. The job was done, and he was home and looking forward to some quiet time with Brian.

His phone vibrated again with another message from Brian. *Dinner to celebrate?*

Nicolai answered *yes* and continued up the walk. His phone vibrated again, and Nicolai looked at the screen, but noticed that the message wasn't from Brian. Huffing, Nicolai looked at the message and saved it like Brian had told him to do, but he still shivered, even on the warm spring evening. *Got a message from Justin,* Nicolai sent to Brian, and he got a response that Brian was leaving the office now and would be there right away.

Nicolai hurried toward the house, looking all around him. That last message from Justin had him a little freaked, and he wanted to get inside. Unlocking the door, Nicolai hurried inside, closing the door hard enough that the vibrations shook through his feet. Nicolai relocked the door and peered out through the curtains. Seeing nothing out of the ordinary, he calmed himself down and settled in to wait for Brian.

A short while later, Nicolai's phone vibrated, and he saw a message from Brian that he would be there in ten minutes. Nicolai watched for his car and opened the door as Brian approached the house. Brian hugged him tight as soon as he was in the house, and Nicolai felt some of his nervousness slip away, his lover's strength and protectiveness soothing his rattled nerves. Brian was here and he wouldn't let anything happen to him.

Sitting in the living room a few minutes later, Nicolai handed Brian his phone and let him see the messages. "On their own, these messages don't seem threatening," Brian told him after looking up. "A court would not understand why these are frightening, but I know they are."

Brian showed him the last message: *I like your blue shirt.*

"How did he know what I was wearing?" Nicolai asked.

"Exactly. He may have seen you at some point today, or he may be watching you. I don't know, but I think it's time we found out. I have a friend, a private investigator, who also happens to be really huge. I want to have him put the fear of God into Justin. Maybe he'll get the message and leave you alone."

Nicolai read Brian's lips and nodded his approval. He'd really thought Justin would move on and leave him alone, but that didn't appear to be the case. "Can we talk about something else?" Nicolai asked, signing his question as well. He and Brian had agreed to try to sign as much of their conversations as possible. Brian found it helpful, since he was still learning, and Nicolai did it out of habit, anyway.

"Okay," Brian signed. "I was notified today that the appeal of Dieter's case has been accepted by the Supreme Court." Brian's signing skills had improved dramatically, and while Brian spelled some words he didn't know, he was doing remarkably well. Nicolai knew it was a sign of just how much Brian cared for him, and that warmed his heart. And Zoe seemed to be picking up on sign language even more quickly than her father.

"Isn't that fast?" Nicolai signed.

"Very fast, but the case has a number of implications that are important. Oral presentations are in late September, but who knows when the court will issue their opinion," Brian told him, and Nicolai gently corrected some of his signs. Brian sometimes made very funny mistakes, but Nicolai had gotten past the point where he commented on them other than as a simple correction.

"In this case, fast is good, I guess." Nicolai certainly hoped so.

"I think so."

"If Dieter wins there, will the Austrians have to return the paintings?"

"Not necessarily. If the Supreme Court rules in our favor, then it will mean that we can sue here in the United States, and that the United States government is bound to enforce the judgment."

"So it could be years yet before he ever gets the paintings?"

"What I'm hoping is that if we win, the Austrians will try to settle. They may offer Dieter the four Pirktl landscapes or the portrait of Anna to settle the case rather than risk losing everything if they lose the case altogether. I haven't asked Dieter how he feels about that, but we'll cross that bridge when we come to it. Right now, I've been taking a course in Supreme Court procedures and protocol. I'm actually rather excited about it. Both Gerald and I are planning to go, and I'm hoping both you and Dieter will go as well."

"Of course I will. Dieter will be a nervous wreck, like he was at the appeal," Nicolai signed. "Has there been much publicity? I never saw anything in the papers."

"Not yet. But there will be now that the appeal has reached this level. One of the news agencies is bound to pick up on it. I've asked

Dieter not to say anything, and we'd choose a reputable organization to speak to when the time comes," Brian explained. "I have to get home soon. Do you want to come home with me? I've missed you these last few weeks." They'd seen each other, but less often than usual because most of Nicolai's weeks had been spent in Chicago.

"I'll pack a bag and be ready to go in a few minutes," Nicolai explained with his hands and fingers before standing up. Brian pulled him into a hug and then angled for a kiss that made Nicolai's toes tingle. "Is that a preview?"

"Yes," Brian answered, and Nicolai hurried upstairs. Packing in a hurry, Nicolai realized just how much he'd missed Brian too. Working in Chicago, his weeks had been long, and by the weekends, when he saw Brian, he was exhausted. Often he'd returned to Chicago on Sunday evening so he could start early on Monday morning. The three days a week they'd thought would be required had turned into five, with Nicolai often doing paperwork on the weekends. But now the project was over, and they had paid him handsomely for his work and expertise. Closing his bag, Nicolai descended the stairs and found Brian standing in the hallway, glaring bullets at Justin.

"I think you should leave and never come back," Nicolai signed once he put down his bag. "I have contacted the police, and your attention is not wanted." Brian had told him once what he should say if he encountered Justin face to face again.

"I just wanted to make sure you were okay."

"By sending me creepy notes all the time?" Nicolai's hands flew as he signed the message, glad that Brian would be able to understand at least some of it. "I don't know what your game is, but I want no part of it."

"Nicolai, I love you," Justin signed.

"That's too bad, because I no longer love you. That was destroyed when you left me. I've found someone else, and he makes me very happy. I love Brian. Not you. So if that isn't plain enough

for you, I don't know what is, but I want you to leave and don't
come back. I don't want any more text messages, and I do not want
you showing up at my house or following me. What we had is over,
and you need to accept that." Nicolai stared into Justin's eyes as he
finished signing, trying to communicate as best he could that he
meant business. "Don't make me get a restraining order, because I
will."

Justin blinked a few times, looking at Brian and then back at
Nicolai. "Is this what you really want?"

"Yes. It's what I wanted three months ago, when I told you to
leave," Nicolai signed in a huff before stepping around Justin to pull
the door open. "Now go!" he said harshly, feeling the words in his
throat. Nicolai waited and saw Justin step outside the house. "Do not
come back." Nicolai closed the door and turned to Brian, who was
smiling at him.

"You were brilliant," Brian signed, and then moved closer.
"Did you mean what you said?" Nicolai blinked a few times.

He'd meant everything he'd said, and it took him a minute to
realize what Brian was referring to. "Yes, I meant it," Nicolai
signed, and almost before he was finished, Brian was kissing him
hard. His man's hands were all over him, and Nicolai forgot about
everything else as Brian told him just what he thought of Nicolai's
declaration. He felt Brian's hands slide down his back, cupping his
butt and then pressing their hips together until Nicolai could feel
Brian's excitement pressing insistently against his hip.

Once Nicolai felt like his knees were going to give out, Brian
broke the kiss, still holding him, looking deep into Nicolai's eyes.
Then he stepped back and made three very deliberate signs: "I.
Love. You." Brian repeated the signs again, and then Nicolai was
held close.

Now it was Nicolai's turn to stop and stare. Yes, he'd told
Brian that he loved him, but he hadn't expected Brian to say it back.
Nicolai had thought that Brian loved him, Brian had certainly shown

it in the way Brian had treated him, but he hadn't expected him to say it. Nicolai sort of felt that Brian was one of those guys who showed his feelings rather than talking about them, and that Brian had actually told Nicolai he loved him was pretty amazing. "You aren't just saying that because I said it, are you?"

Brian backed away and shook his head, locking their eyes together. Then Nicolai felt a light touch on his chin before Brian again made the signs for "I love you." Nicolai made the same signs and then smiled. "We have to meet Zoe," Brian said, and Nicolai looked down at his bag.

"What about Zoe? How is she going to feel about this?" Brian had always been very careful around his daughter, and other than the one time, they'd never spent the night together when she was around.

"I had a talk with her. Not *the talk*, but sort of a pre-sex-talk talk. She told me she already knows where babies come from." Brian smiled, and Nicolai figured this was going to be good. "She said that 'when a mommy and a daddy decide to make a baby, they go into the bedroom, take off their clothes, and then ka-boomba-boomba-boomba, nine months later, out pops junior.'"

Nicolai wasn't sure he understood and had Brian repeat it. Then they both broke down laughing. "That's not the best part," Brian added once they calmed down. "She then said, 'Daddy, it's okay if you and Nicolai want to ka-boomba-boomba-boomba, just don't expect to make any babies.'"

That time Nicolai knew he'd understood. "She does not miss much, does she?" he signed, and he saw Brian smile as he shook his head. "I think we better go before Zoe and Georgia wonder if something has happened."

Brian nodded his head yes and opened the door, holding it while Nicolai walked outside into the fresh spring evening. After making sure the door was locked, Nicolai followed Brian to his car and got in the passenger seat. They rode to Brian's house in their usual quiet, but the entire way all Nicolai could think about was ka-boomba-boomba-boomba.

When they arrived at Brian's, Nicolai got out of the car and carried his bag inside, putting it in Brian's bedroom. Then he found Brian and Zoe in the media room with Georgia. They seemed to be laughing and having a good time. Once she saw him, Zoe hurried over, giving him a hug and pulling him in with the rest of them. Zoe refused to sit still until she had told Nicolai about all the new signs she'd learned, and he found her absolutely amazing.

"What do you want for dinner?" Brian signed, and Zoe responded with "chicken nuggets" and then changed her mind and signed "pizza." Nicolai saw Brian pull out his phone and figured he was ordering dinner, while Zoe tugged and pointed to the game she already had set up.

"Do you want a rematch?" Nicolai asked with his hands, and Zoe grinned, nodding vigorously before handing him a controller. Zoe started the game and the race was off. They played through the entire series, with Zoe finishing right behind him. It had been mostly luck, but she celebrated right along with him, with Georgia joining in as well. Then Zoe coerced Georgia and Brian to play. Georgia creamed Brian in every race, but he appeared good-natured about it, and eventually he left the room when the doorbell rang, returning with two pizza boxes, plates, glasses, and drinks. They ate, played, and ate some more until the pizza was gone and Nicolai's fingers hurt from pressing the game buttons over and over again.

Georgia said good-bye to all of them, including giving Nicolai a hug that he hadn't been expecting, and left. Eventually Zoe changed the game to some sort of dancing thing where you had to mimic the movements on the screen. Nicolai sat back and watched as Zoe did really well. He had no idea what she was dancing to, but Zoe seemed to have a ball. The best part was that Brian sat with him as they watched Zoe having what looked like the time of her life. Nicolai saw Brian say something to Zoe, and she changed the game again, this time to tennis, and they again took turns. Brian excelled at this game and wiped the floor with both of them.

When it was time for Zoe to go to bed, she hugged both Brian and Nicolai good night and then left the room. Nicolai knew she was getting ready for bed. When Brian left as well, Nicolai sat alone on the sofa. He could hardly believe the day he'd had—Brian had actually told him that he loved him.

Nicolai didn't notice Brian's return until he felt him sit on the sofa. Then he was hugged and held against Brian's strong, warm body, and Nicolai let himself go, enjoying the sensation of being held, and for that matter, loved. Angling his head so he could see Brian's eyes, he was kissed softly. Nicolai let his eyes drift closed as Brian continued to kiss him, his mind and body floating on the sweetness of his lover's taste.

When Brian pulled back, Nicolai didn't try to speak to him, he didn't think words were necessary, and Brian seemed to agree. After standing up, Brian held out his hand, and Nicolai took it, allowing himself to be led to the bedroom. Nicolai sat on the edge of the bed, looking at Brian, who held up a single finger and then left the room, returning a minute later and closing the door. Brian stepped to him, eyes filled with emotion. Nicolai wondered what Brian was doing when he didn't come close, but then Nicolai saw him slowly move his arms as he once again signed, "I love you," this time using his whole body, making the simple signs as expressive as Nicolai could ever have imagined.

Brian seemed to float to him, their lips touching, gentle pressure bending him back on the bed. Nicolai held Brian tight, and their kisses deepened quickly, Brian's tongue taking possession of his mouth. When his lips moved away, Nicolai made an attempt to follow, but Brian had other ideas. Brian tugged off Nicolai's shirt, tossing it aside before warm lips touched his skin. Nicolai loved the way Brian seemed to worship him, like he was the most important person on earth. Every touch and caress seemed to set Nicolai on fire. Brian was being so gentle and caring, but what Nicolai really wanted right now was a little wildness.

Slipping from beneath Brian, Nicolai decided that he needed to take control. Brian might love to be in charge in the court room, but in the bedroom, he'd shown a willingness to let Nicolai take charge. Brian watched him, his eyes widening, as Nicolai climbed off the bed. First, he shimmied out of his pants before prowling naked around the bed. Brian stared at him, so Nicolai moved in, tugging off his shirt while Brian slipped out of his shoes.

Nicolai felt Brian's hands on his skin, but he didn't let those sweet caresses distract him from his prey. Parting Brian's pants, he tugged them down his legs before casting them aside. Then he pounced, leaping at Brian. They fell together on the bed, with Nicolai kissing Brian ravenously. He couldn't get enough of his lover right now—Brian had said he loved him, and that fueled his passion like gasoline on a fire.

Brian seemed to love what Nicolai was doing, and after he got Brian settled on the bed, Nicolai proceeded to devour him. Nipples, neck, stomach, chest, legs—nothing was spared from his tongue and lips. Nicolai hadn't touched Brian's cock, and already the man was writhing on the bed so energetically that Nicolai could feel it shaking beneath them. Nicolai saw Brian's lips moving, but he couldn't make out what he was saying, so Nicolai imagined he was begging for his lips and for his touch. Nicolai decided it was time to give his lover what he wanted. Settling between Brian's legs, Nicolai ran his lips down Brian's length and felt Brian's hips thrust slightly.

Spreading Brian's legs with his body, Nicolai took Brian deep as he slipped a finger behind Brian's balls, circling his tight opening. Brian's thrusting increased, and Nicolai took that as a good sign as he licked his fingers. Teasing the puckered skin, Nicolai slipped a wet finger into his lover's body and felt Brian still. Nicolai let Brian slip from his lips as he looked into Brian's eyes, making sure his advance was welcome. It seemed to be, and slowly, Nicolai added a second finger, Brian's body gripping him hard. Nicolai might not have been able to *hear* Brian's reaction, but Nicolai was very good at reading people's reactions, and he knew from the way Brian's body throbbed and the way his head rolled back and forth on the pillow that he was enjoying what Nicolai was doing.

Taking Brian in his mouth again, Nicolai sucked hard as he wriggled his fingers inside Brian's body, and the results seemed to electrify Brian. His hips thrust, and Nicolai could feel him trying to get Nicolai's fingers deeper into his body.

Letting Brian's cock slip from his lips, Nicolai withdrew his fingers before kneeling between Brian's legs and locking onto his lover's eyes. He needed to know what Brian wanted, and he wasn't sure how to ask. He and Justin had always had defined roles in bed, with each knowing what the other expected, but this was new, and Nicolai knew that what he was asking was very new to Brian.

Brian reached to the bedside table and handed Nicolai a condom. Nicolai swallowed, knowing the trust that Brian was showing at that moment.

"I love you," Nicolai said, feeling a lump forming in his throat. Opening the packet, Nicolai rolled it down his length, and Brian handed him a small bottle. After coating both himself and Brian, Nicolai slowly entered Brian's body for the first time. He knew he had to go slow and watch for any signs of discomfort. Nicolai saw Brian grit his teeth a few times. Stopping, he waited until Brian seemed ready again before pressing deeper into Brian's amazingly tight body. The hottest heat Nicolai had ever experienced surrounded him as he sank fully into Brian, his lover throbbing and gripping him like a vise.

Leaning forward, Nicolai brought Brian's lips to his as he waited for his lover to adjust to the new sensations. Then, slowly, Nicolai began to move. Nicolai knew each and every sensation was new for Brian, and he also knew that each guy was different. Since he could hear no vocal cues regarding what Brian liked, Nicolai let his lover's body guide him. When Brian tensed, Nicolai slowed down, and when he relaxed and Nicolai could see his breathing, deep and full, he sped up.

Brian's eyes stared up at him, and Nicolai consciously maintained contact. He knew more than anyone that the eyes were indeed the window to the soul, and as their lovemaking progressed, Nicolai felt as though he were seeing deeper and deeper into Brian—like he was stripping away all the layers until Brian's very soul was laid out for him and Nicolai could see it all through Brian's amazing eyes. Nicolai felt his heart swell at the love and happiness that shone out from Brian's eyes, but seemed to originate from within Brian's very soul.

Nicolai's breath caught when he saw Brian's hands move, making the signs for "I love you" while they made love. He stopped moving altogether, buried deep within his lover, connected deeply and totally. Nicolai tried to make the signs in return, but Brian's sentiments had put him off balance and he couldn't, so Nicolai let his actions and touch convey his feelings as they made love.

At some point, Nicolai realized that he was speaking, though he also realized he wasn't sure what he'd been saying, but whatever it was seemed to make Brian very happy because he pulled him down into a deep kiss that threatened to blow Nicolai's mind. Their bodies joined, combined with Brian's deep kisses and the heady feeling of his lover's skin against his, had Nicolai flying. Every movement of Brian's body around him sent tiny electric shocks up and down his spine. He reveled in the decadent sight of Brian lying on his back beneath him, feet resting on Nicolai's shoulders, eyes half-lidded, head rocking slowly back and forth on the pillow. Brian looked to be in total ecstasy, and Nicolai knew he was the man driving him there. That feeling propelled Nicolai forward, driving deep into Brian's body as his tenuous hold on the last of his control began to slip. And when Brian crossed his arms over his chest, holding them there, making the sign for love, Nicolai completely lost it, coming hard, his mouth hanging open. Nicolai tried to watch his lover, but the sensation was just too great, and his eyes clamped closed as his release barreled through him.

Once his body stopped throbbing and his mind began to function again, Nicolai opened his eyes and saw Brian shaking beneath him, his body rigidly tight. Replacing Brian's hand with his, Nicolai stroked Brian until he came, shooting his release over Nicolai's hand and up along his own chest.

Nicolai slipped from Brian's body, and he tugged off the condom, hurrying to dispose of it before returning with a cloth. After a cleanup, Nicolai climbed back in bed, holding Brian tight. Nicolai knew he didn't speak much unless he had something to say. With Justin, they had never made small talk in bed. Nicolai had never felt the need, but now he began to talk. He hoped he wasn't too loud. Volume was very hard, if not nearly impossible, but it was one of the things he'd practiced with his computer program, and he'd learned how various volumes of speech felt in his throat.

Brian rolled them on the bed, and Nicolai found himself looking up into Brian's face. "You are so beautiful," Brian signed before kissing him hard. "I love how you try to do things for me." Brian kissed him once again. "I love you very much."

"I love you too," Nicolai signed back.

"I want to ask you something, and it's important. I was going to ask you earlier, but I want to ask you now, after we've made love, so you know I'm serious," Nicolai saw Brian say, Brian's eyes locking on his for emphasis. "I have been thinking about this for a while, and I want to ask if you'll come live with me? Live with us, here."

Nicolai was floored. He had not been expecting that question, at least not yet. "I would love to live with you, but not yet," Nicolai said as he signed, and he saw the smile fade from Brian's face. "I love you very much, but you just came out, and Zoe needs a chance to get used to who you are without me around all the time. You also have an ex-wife who has to come to terms with your being gay."

"What does she have to do with us?" Nicolai read on Brian's lips as he saw hurt flash in Brian's eyes.

"She's Zoe's mother and she could make trouble for you. I'm not saying no, because I want to live with you," Nicolai added, signing and talking as fast as he could. "I'm simply saying we should take things slow and let other people catch up to us. Zoe needs to see us together so she can understand what we mean to each other, and so I can build a relationship with her that is based on something more than video-game tournaments." The disappointment in Brian's eyes tore at Nicolai's heart, and his hands faltered. He hated to disappoint Brian, and he was tempted to say yes just to make him happy, but Nicolai didn't feel as though that was the right thing to do.

"Are you scared of something?" Brian signed, and Nicolai nodded his head on the pillow.

"I've fallen totally in love with you, and I'm scared you'll wake up and realize that you could have your pick of any man you meet, or that you'll decide you don't want—" Nicolai couldn't proceed with what he was saying. He didn't want to even say what he feared most. Being in a relationship with someone who was deaf was difficult, especially for a person with normal hearing. Nicolai knew he could easily come to rely on Brian. Hell, he already had for some things and it frightened him, because what if Brian wasn't always there and he had to go back to relying fully on himself. He'd relied on Justin for years, and it had taken him awhile to regain skills he'd let lapse because he hadn't needed them. He didn't want that to happen again.

Brian's hand caressed along his cheek and then his hand slipped away. "I will not get tired of you. Yes, being with you requires extra effort, but you are worth it." Brian kissed him hard once he was done speaking. Nicolai knew he was sincere, and it warmed his heart, but he also knew he was right. They needed more time.

"We will talk about this some more," Brian said once he broke the kiss, and Nicolai nodded, happy he hadn't messed everything up. Slowly, Brian settled on the bed, and Nicolai tensed. He half expected Brian to roll over and go right to sleep—Justin had always done that whenever Nicolai had disappointed him. But instead, Nicolai felt Brian hug him close, his lover's chest pressing to Nicolai's back, a hand lightly caressing his tummy. Brian gently kissed his neck, and Nicolai knew he hadn't blown it and that everything would be all right, at least for now.

CHAPTER 7

THE last few weeks had been hectic, to say the least. With the initial preparations for the appearance before the Supreme Court as well as fighting with Barbara about taking Zoe to Vienna for a week, Brian had been exhausted by the time he got both Zoe and himself packed with their passports and all the appropriate documentation. He'd actually had to increase her alimony for a month in order to get Barbara to agree to let Zoe go, but it had been worth it to see Zoe's excitement about her first plane ride. Somehow, the night before they were to leave, Brian got Zoe into bed, and then he and Nicolai went to bed as well. Neither of them slept, and judging by Zoe's lack of energy, she didn't either.

Once they boarded the huge plane in Chicago for their transatlantic flight, Zoe lasted through dinner before falling asleep in her seat, with her pillowed head resting against Nicolai. She didn't wake up again until they served breakfast before landing. Nicolai might have been right about using caution regarding his relationship with Zoe, but it seemed as though his daughter had her own ideas. She glommed onto him for almost the entire trip and even acted as his interpreter sometimes, to both Nicolai's and Brian's delight. At one point just before dinner, one of the flight attendants offered Nicolai a drink, and since he was looking away, he didn't realize the flight attendant was there.

Zoe looked up from the picture she was coloring. "He can't hear you, he's deaf," Zoe answered politely, and tapped Nicolai on the shoulder.

"I said, 'Would you like something to drink?'" the male flight attendant said firmly, almost at the top of his lungs.

Brian was about to say something when Zoe beat him to it. "He's deaf, not stupid," Zoe retorted with her patented eye roll before signing the message to Nicolai, who seemed completely oblivious. Once Nicolai had answered, she returned to her coloring as though nothing had happened, and Brian reminded himself that he needed to have a talk with her about behaving properly, but he couldn't do it then because Brian knew he'd never get through the talk with a straight face.

He and Nicolai hadn't talked any more about living together, but Brian hadn't forgotten, and the more time passed, the more his heart knew what it wanted. During the flight, Nicolai fell asleep as well, and Brian, who was never able to sleep on a plane, spent an hour watching his lover sleep. Nicolai was adorable, curled under his blanket, Zoe still using him as a prop for her pillow. They looked like two absolute angels, and they were his, both of them. His daughter and Nicolai, the two people he loved most in the world. As he'd watched, Nicolai's eyes had fluttered open for a few seconds, Brian had smiled at him, and Nicolai had taken his hand, holding it as his eyes drifted closed again.

After landing, they located Gerald and Dieter, who had been in a completely different section of the plane. They hadn't been able to get seats together, so Brian, Nicolai, and Zoe had been seated near the back of the plane, while Dieter and Gerald had been seated a good twenty or thirty rows ahead of them. Once they deplaned, Brian carried Zoe through the airport, and while they waited in the line for passport control, she nearly fell back to sleep with her head resting on his shoulder. That ended as soon as they made their way into the subway system, and by the time they reached the area of the city where they were staying, Zoe was wide awake and her usual bundle of energy.

"This is where Uncle Dieter's great-grandparents used to live," Brian explained to Zoe as they entered the front door of the grand building. It still retained a lot of its stately elegance. They followed Gerald and Dieter inside and let Dieter speak with the gentleman behind the desk. He seemed to recognize Dieter, and after they had signed the guest registry and handed over their credit cards and passports, the man showed them up the grand staircase to their second-floor rooms.

Brian had booked what they referred to as a small suite because it contained a separate small bedroom. The room was exquisite. Brian and Nicolai set down the bags, and Zoe raced to the other room, squealing with delight at the puffy pink bedspread and décor perfect for a little girl. Brian heard a knock and opened the door to Gerald and a rather shaken Dieter.

"What is it?" Brian asked as he motioned for them to come inside.

"Can Dieter look around?" Gerald asked, and Brian nodded. "Our room used to be his Gram's bedroom."

Dieter stopped his slow progress around the room. "Gram told me that when she was a girl, she and a friend had once carved their names in the molding inside the doorframe of her closet, sort of a 'friends forever' thing, and I found it."

"Are you going to be okay staying here?" Brian asked, as Nicolai, not hearing what was being said, but sensing something was wrong, moved to hug his friend.

"Yes. I guess I hadn't realized what this place would mean to me. When we were in Vienna the last time, it didn't mean much, but finding Gram's name has made this place come alive." Dieter pushed open the curtains and peered out the windows that overlooked the back garden. "This was Anna's room," Dieter explained quietly, looking at Nicolai, whose eyes widened. Zoe wandered into the room, and Brian saw her look at everyone before rushing to her Uncle Dieter.

"I'm okay, Zoe," Dieter reassured her as he wiped his eyes. "I just hadn't expected for this to be this emotional an experience. Anyway, we need to get something to eat, and then we can start having some fun."

"Yay!" Zoe cried enthusiastically. "I wanna see where the princess lives."

"There isn't a princess anymore," Dieter explained, "but there is a palace, and we can go through it if you want. In fact, there are two palaces, and we can see both of them. We can also take a carriage ride and go to an amusement park and all kinds of stuff. But we can't do it all today." Dieter seemed happier, with some of Zoe's energy rubbing off on him. After a little more discussion, they got ready to leave and found a restaurant for a light lunch, with Dieter convincing Zoe that chicken schnitzel was chicken nuggets pounded flat. She didn't seem convinced at first, but after a taste wolfed down half the serving.

They spent the rest of the day taking the Sissy Tour of the Hofburg Palace, much to Zoe's delight. Sissy had been the last empress. Brian signed and mouthed what the tour guide said as best he could for Nicolai so he wouldn't be completely lost. It wasn't smooth, but Nicolai said it seemed to work fairly well.

"Daddy, will you get me diamond stars for my hair like Sissy had?" Zoe asked as she peered into the display of the last empress's signature star-shaped hair decorations.

"You'd be very pretty, but you're not a princess," Brian explained, hoping he'd dodged that bullet.

"But you always said I was your princess." Brian didn't know what to say to that, and thankfully, when they got to the gift shop, there were indeed stars made out of crystal. Brian broke down and bought her one while both Gerald and Dieter wagged their pinkies at him. After Brian paid for it, Nicolai helped her put it into her hair. Brian had to admit, she did look beautiful.

After leaving the palace, they continued walking and looking around before getting dinner and heading back to the hotel. Zoe went right to bed, with Brian and Nicolai following right behind. Falling into the bed, Brian only had enough energy to pull Nicolai close before closing his eyes and letting sleep take him.

In the morning, they got cleaned up and met Dieter and Gerald for breakfast. Zoe must have slept well because she woke with an amazing amount of energy. They all decided to take her to the park, where they could run and play before visiting the museum. By the time they stopped for lunch, Zoe was still going, and the only people tired were the adults. After a lunch of what Zoe called schnitzel nuggets, among other things, the group headed over to the museum.

Brian held Zoe's hand as they wandered from gallery to gallery, turning the room after room of art into a game for the nine-year-old that degenerated into what could only be termed "find the boobies."

"When are we going to see Uncle Dieter's grandma?" Zoe asked when she tired of the game.

"It's his great-grandmother, and we should get there very soon," Brian explained as they walked into the room with four Pirktl landscapes, and even Zoe stopped and looked at the paintings. She'd lost interest a while ago, but these four works of art caught even her attention.

Nicolai took Brian's arm, and the three of them stared at the depictions of the four seasons that almost seemed to be in motion. But the most amazing thing was the effect they had on Dieter. He stood in the middle of the gallery and looked from one to the next, and when he reached the last one, he started again. Nicolai's grip tightened as they looked at the paintings and then watched Dieter look at the paintings. Eventually, Gerald said something to Dieter, and he nodded before moving on.

Brian hadn't known what to expect when he saw the portrait of Anna, but when he entered the gallery and saw *The Woman in Blue* for the first time, he stepped back, because he almost felt as though she were looking into his heart. "Have you seen this before?" Brian signed to Nicolai, and he shook his head.

"Only pictures," he answered with his hands before turning back to the portrait. Even Zoe stood stark still for a few minutes before getting antsy.

"Daddy, what's wrong with Uncle Dieter?" Zoe whispered, and Brian looked at Dieter and saw a tear running down his face. Brian had no idea what Dieter was feeling, but the portrait moved Brian even apart from it being Dieter's ancestor. For Dieter, he could only imagine the experience must have been profoundly moving.

Brian knelt so he could look Zoe in the eyes. "The picture of his great-grandmother touches him very deeply."

"Is he sad?"

"It's hard to describe, but maybe he is a little sad, yes. Why don't you go give him a hug? Maybe he'll feel better." Brian smiled at her, and she strode over to Uncle Dieter and was lifted into his arms, where she hugged him tight.

Brian felt a hand slide into his, and he looked into Nicolai's huge, watery eyes. "We have to get this painting for Dieter. Somehow, we have to win. He even looks like her, and we just have to get her back for him." Nicolai moved into Brian's arms. "We just have to."

Brian knew that Nicolai was right. He was a lawyer and he'd seen people fight over possession of a cheap plastic figurine for months simply because it would hurt someone else. He'd also seen so much greed over the years that he was totally jaded when it came to lawsuits. Even after all these months working with Gerald and Dieter, Brian realized that he'd been treating this lawsuit like any other. Granted, that was part of doing a good job and keeping himself detached so he could do his job well.

But as he stood watching Dieter in the gallery, he realized something Nicolai and Gerald had known all along: this wasn't just another case. This was something special. Dieter wasn't after these paintings because of how much they were worth, and Dieter wasn't counting how much money he could get once he sold them. These paintings represented so much more to his friend. They represented Dieter's family. He'd never known Anna and Joseph, and Dieter had never really known his parents. Even his grandmother was gone, so these paintings represented a connection to Dieter's family, to an empty place in Dieter's heart. Winning this case was about justice, pure and simple. It wasn't about money, but returning something special and amazing to the person who would love and cherish them more than anyone else in the world.

When Dieter had given him the etching, no matter what he'd told Nicolai, Brian hadn't realized the full impact of what the younger man was telling him. Brian swallowed when he realized that Dieter didn't just consider Nicolai his brother, but maybe he considered Brian one as well. That thought sent goose bumps up his spine, and Nicolai shifted next to him. Brian looked at Nicolai and mouthed, "I know. I'll do my very best."

With the exception of Georgia, Brian's own family was difficult at best. His mother seemed to be coming around, but Brian barely spoke to his father, and that was before the revelation that he was gay. But standing in this gallery were people who accepted him for who he was and loved him. Brian let his gaze shift back to the painting and then to Dieter, who was now talking softly with Zoe and Gerald, his emotions under control. These people were his family, the one he'd made and chosen, or maybe they'd chosen him, which was an even nicer thought.

"I think we're ready to go," Dieter told them as they approached. They were no longer alone, and Brian noticed that other people were looking at Dieter and then at the portrait of Anna. The resemblance was striking. "I don't want to pose for pictures today." Gerald, Dieter, and Zoe left the gallery, and Brian listened as his daughter's voice got softer.

"Are you ready?" Nicolai signed, and Brian shook his head, taking a last look at the portrait. She seemed to be speaking to him. Brian wondered what she said to other people, but to him she seemed to be saying, "Bring me home."

"Let's go," Brian signed, and he let Nicolai lead him back through the galleries. They found the others back in the gallery with the landscapes, and Brian listened as Dieter explained the paintings to Zoe. "They're all the same set of trees, and this one is summer. Can you see how the trees look like they're fanning themselves because it's so hot?" Dieter asked her, and Zoe nodded slowly. When she saw him, Zoe hurried toward him, pulling him over to repeat what Dieter had told her.

Brian half listened, his mind whirling with all the things he'd realized in the last few minutes. "Daddy," Zoe whined slightly, and Brian slipped out of his thoughts. "Can we do something fun now?"

Her Uncle Dieter scooped Zoe off her feet. "Yes, we can. Let's get on the subway and go to the Prater."

"What's a Prater?" Zoe asked as they left the gallery and made their way back toward the entrance of the museum. Brian slipped his arm around Nicolai's waist, following the others. He had so much he wanted to talk over with him, but they needed to be alone. So he filed the questions away for after Zoe was asleep.

A few people looked at them funny when they saw his arm around Nicolai, but Brian glared back at them, and they looked away. Outside in the fresh air and sunshine, Brian felt some of the nearly oppressive level of emotion begin to lift. "Before we leave this area, let's see if we can get tickets to the Royal Lipizzaner Stallion show," Gerald suggested.

"What are those?" Zoe asked hopefully.

"It's a show with beautiful royal horses," Brian explained. Gerald consulted the map he kept in his pack, and they walked through the maze of buildings to the ticket booth. The stallions were part of the Hofburg Palace complex, and they were able to get tickets for a show the day before they were scheduled to leave.

"Can we have fun now?" Zoe asked.

"Yes," Dieter answered her with a grin. "We're going to the subway now." Zoe giggled when Dieter tickled her. Once her laughter died down, Zoe ran to Brian, walking between him and Nicolai, taking each of their hands.

Reaching the subway, Brian held Zoe's hand until they were seated in the subway car, and after a short ride, they exited and climbed the stairs up to ground level. The first thing Zoe saw was the massive antique Ferris wheel, and she practically pulled Brian toward it to get him to walk faster. "Can we go on that?" Zoe asked as she pointed toward the huge wheel with large enclosed cabins.

"Are you sure? It's pretty tall," Brian cautioned.

"Yes, Daddy, yes," Zoe cried with a grin.

"Then Dieter and I will take you if your dad's too scared," Gerald chided him with a smile as he and Zoe raced ahead, their laughter drifting back.

"Gerald and I will take Zoe," Dieter told Brian softly. "You and Nicolai go in a car on your own. It's very romantic." Dieter winked at him and then raced away to catch up to Zoe and Gerald.

Brian looked at Nicolai, who smiled warmly back at him. So far the city had been magical, and in the late-afternoon sun, with the sounds of laughter building as they approached the Prater entrance, Brian felt like a kid again, happy, excited, and in love.

"Would you like to ride?" Brian asked, pointing to the wheel, and Nicolai nodded. They got in line and saw Zoe with her uncles at the front of the line. She waved as they disappeared into their car, and Brian watched as the wheel began to spin. Their turn came and they got into the large cabin. The attendant closed the door and they began to move. Higher and higher they rose, Brian and Nicolai sitting next to each other on the bench. For a total of two seconds, he watched the view, that is, until he felt Nicolai's hand on his cheek. Brian turned to face Nicolai, who kissed him hard, almost possessively, and Brian really liked it when Nicolai took charge. Brian felt Nicolai's weight shift, and he slid even closer on the bench.

The cabin began to descend, and Nicolai continued kissing him, letting Brian up only when they passed through the station. As soon as they were out in the sun again, Nicolai looked deeply into Brian's eyes and growled. Brian knew Nicolai had no idea he was making any sound at all, but damn if that didn't turn him on. They really hadn't had much time alone since they'd arrived in Vienna, so Nicolai's kisses and the way his hand slithered under Brian's shirt drove him completely insane. Their cabin began to descend once more, and Nicolai gentled his kisses before letting him up. Somehow Brian managed to put himself back together as the riders were switched in the cabin in front of them.

When the attendant opened the door, they saw Dieter, Gerald, and Zoe waiting for them. Zoe looked excited, while both Dieter and Gerald wore "we know what you've been doing" expressions. Brian waited for Nicolai to step off, and Zoe rushed to him, practically tugging Nicolai after her. Once they'd all exited, Zoe pointed toward a huge roller-coaster. "Will you take me on that?" she asked Nicolai, and he shook his head.

"My balance isn't good enough. I will get sick," Nicolai explained.

"I'll take you, squirt," Dieter told her, and Brian nodded when he saw Dieter look at him for permission. "The old folks need their rest," he added, to Zoe's delight, and they mimicked walking with canes for a few moments before taking off hand in hand toward the coaster. Brian had no interest, but he could see Gerald was trying to decide if he wanted to brave it or not.

"Go on and have fun. Nicolai and I will wait for you."

Gerald followed Dieter and Zoe to buy tickets while Nicolai and Brian found a bench.

"You could have gone," Nicolai signed, and Brian shook his head vehemently, making a motion to indicate he'd get sick, too, and Nicolai nodded knowingly. Actually, Brian could ride roller-coasters all day long, but he was simply grateful for a few minutes to sit quietly with his lover.

Brian listened to the laughter, screams of joy, as well as the sounds of the rides, people talking, the wind in the trees, birds squawking, and thought that Nicolai could hear none of it. He'd once tried to find out what it was like not being able to hear, but he couldn't block out all the sound. What would it be like to live in a silent world? Brian couldn't imagine it, the same as he couldn't begin to understand what it must be like for Nicolai to have once known sound and lost the ability to hear. Brian touched Nicolai's arm to get his attention. "Is there anything that could be done to allow you to hear again?" Brian signed as best he could, hoping he didn't mess up the signs.

Nicolai looked confused. "No. I used to hope that something would be developed, sort of an artificial ear, but I gave up on that a long time ago. Why?"

"I've wondered what it would be like for you to be able to hear again. I've tried to imagine what it would be like not to be able to hear, and I can't."

"If my hearing came back all at once, it would drive me crazy because I'm used to silence now," Nicolai explained as he signed. "Not that I wouldn't like to hear again, but it's not going to happen, and I accepted that a long time ago. I am who I am, and it took me a long time to get where I can accept myself and love myself for who I am."

Brian scooted closer to Nicolai, turning to face him. "Don't get me wrong, that's one of the things I admire most about you. I wish I could be as happy in my own skin as you seem to be." So many things in his life seemed to be up in the air right now.

"We all find our way. Some of us do it a little later than others, that's all." Nicolai seemed relieved, and Brian wondered why. "When you asked about my hearing again, I thought…."

"You thought I was getting tired of being in a relationship with a deaf person," Brian finished, and Nicolai nodded sheepishly. "Your being deaf is a part of who you are, and I don't want you to change. I was just curious." So many things about Nicolai fascinated him, but his upbeat attitude and the fact that he never let anything stop him topped the list.

Brian saw Zoe racing toward them, dodging around people before launching herself into his lap. "That was so cool, Daddy. Uncle Dieter took me on it twice. Uncle Gerald looked like he was gonna woof, so he only went on it once."

Dieter and Gerald followed behind her. Gerald did indeed look a little shaken, and Brian got up so Gerald could sit down a few minutes. "It looks like I made the right decision."

"It was like riding an eggbeater. I'll be fine in a few minutes," Gerald explained after sitting down. "Dieter and Zoe loved it, though. I think we can find a place to get dinner as soon as the world stops spinning," Gerald teased before getting back on his feet. "Let's find a place to eat. I'll be fine in a few minutes."

"Are you gonna woof, Uncle Gerald?" Zoe asked expectantly.

"No," he answered and threw her a look that made Zoe giggle. "Let's find one of these beer gardens. Once my stomach settles, I think I'm going to be thirsty." Gerald tickled Zoe, and she wriggled in his arms as they headed off toward one of the many outdoor restaurants.

Entering, they were shown to a table beneath trees lit with fairy lights. Zoe looked all around as they took their seats. Once they received their menus and placed drink orders, Brian's phone began to ring. Getting up from the table, he stepped to a quiet place to answer it. "This is Brian Watson." There weren't many people who'd be calling him.

"Brian, it's Harold," the senior partner at the law firm said. "Linda just informed me that your ex-wife filed a suit for custody of Zoe." Brian felt as though the wind had just been knocked out of his chest. "I know you're on vacation," Harold continued, "but I figured you'd want to know. Linda says she has everything under control, and you know her—she's like a bulldog, especially where children are concerned."

"Tell her this is probably a ploy to get more alimony. She doesn't really want any more time with Zoe. She never makes use of the time she has," Brian said, seething inside. "Also tell Linda to find out about a man who, according to Zoe, is having sleepovers with her." Brian tried to keep his brain from short-circuiting. *How low could Barbara get?* "I'm assuming the basis of this suit is my sexuality."

"That's what's in the papers she filed. It won't go very far," Harold told him. "I really didn't want to disturb you. But we thought you needed to know. Try to have fun and don't worry about a thing. Linda will handle everything from this end."

"Call me if anything changes," Brian said, and Harold promised he would before telling Brian to say hello to everyone. He disconnected the call and walked back toward the table.

"What's wrong?" Nicolai signed to him almost as soon as he saw him.

"I'll tell you later," he signed back, grateful that Zoe was occupied by Dieter.

"We ordered you a Weissbier, and hopefully our server will be back soon to take our orders," Gerald told him, and Brian tasted his beer, letting the cold drink wash down some of the anxiety he was feeling. As a lawyer, he knew in his mind that Barbara didn't have much of a case, but all Zoe needed was more disruption in her life.

She had done remarkably well in school and seemed happy. At least Brian hoped she was happy. What Barbara probably wanted was money, and he was tempted to give it to her to get her to leave them alone.

"Penny for your thoughts," Dieter said as he looked at him from across the table, and Brian shook his head. He really didn't want to talk about this in front of Zoe. She didn't need to know just what a selfish, greedy bitch her mother was. "You seem a million miles away," Dieter added, "did something happen?"

Brian leaned his head toward Zoe, and the boys got the message. Thankfully, the conversation shifted around him, though try as he might, Brian couldn't pay attention. He was too lost in his own worries.

Nicolai's hand touched Brian's leg, squeezing slightly, reassuringly. "Dieter, would you take Zoe for a walk for a minute?" Nicolai asked, and Zoe bounded off her chair and back out into the midway. "Now, what's going on?" Nicolai signed, and Brian turned so Nicolai could read his lips. "Barbara filed suit for custody of Zoe. That was my office. She knew I was on vacation, and she did it on purpose. She's claiming that because I'm gay, I'm not fit to raise Zoe. I know she's just after an increase in her alimony, and the only reason she wants Zoe is for child support, which she won't use for Zoe but for herself. The case doesn't really have much to stand on, but it's still upsetting."

"Is Linda handling it for you?" Gerald asked, and Brian nodded. "Then don't worry about it. She's the best, and it wouldn't surprise me if she has her shut down before we get home. She's damned good—scary, but good. I know it's easier said than done, but don't let it ruin your vacation. None of us are going to let anything happen to our Zoe."

Nicolai nodded his agreement. "She's very special, and I'll throttle your ex-wife myself if she hurts that little girl."

"Hurts what little girl?" Zoe asked as she hurried to the table, and Brian pulled her onto his lap.

"It's nothing. Do you know what you want to eat?"

Zoe nodded. "Flat chicken nuggets." As if everyone at the table didn't know. They all looked over the menu and placed their orders when the server returned. Brian did his best to not let the call ruin the evening, and once Zoe returned to her seat, Nicolai's hand found its way to his leg and stayed there as if Nicolai were showing him he was there and that Brian wasn't alone. Even when he'd been married, he'd always felt somewhat alone, but with Nicolai and the rest of what he was coming to regard as his extended family, he was realizing he had people on his side, and it felt good.

Brian did his best to keep his worries at bay for the rest of dinner. Once they left the restaurant, Zoe dragged them through the rest of the Prater until she was nearly dead on her feet. When they decided it was time to leave, they walked back to the subway. By the time they reached the hotel, Zoe was half-asleep, and after cleaning up, she crawled into bed and asked Brian if they could go back to the rides before they left. When Brian told her yes, she hugged him and was asleep almost before her head hit the pillow.

After leaving Zoe's little room, Brian left the door cracked slightly before joining Nicolai in their room.

"Do you want to talk about it?" Nicolai asked, and Brian shook his head. There really wasn't much to say. He didn't know anything more than what Harold had told him, and there probably wouldn't be much movement before they returned home. There was nothing he could do except try not to let it ruin their vacation. Wandering through the room, Brian felt a bit like a caged animal. He wanted to be doing something, in spite of the fact that there was nothing he could actually do. Brian saw Nicolai walk to Zoe's door, peering inside for a second before closing it silently. Then Nicolai switched off the lights, except for a single small light on the desk. Going into the bathroom, he closed the door. Brian continued pacing and thinking, wondering if there was anything else he could do to help Linda.

The bathroom door opened, and Nicolai stepped out wearing his robe and carrying his clothes. Looking at Brian sternly, he pointed to the bathroom, and Brian nodded before walking into the bathroom, closing the door. After cleaning up and using the facilities, Brian stripped out of his clothes and decided to take a shower, hoping it would help calm his mind. Starting the water, Brian stepped in and washed quickly before letting the water sluice over him. Realizing it wasn't helping, Brian stepped out and dried himself before pulling on the robe Nicolai had left out for him. Opening the door, Brian saw Nicolai resting on the bed waiting for him, and as soon as he saw Brian, Nicolai patted the bed next to him.

Stripping off the robe, Brian found a pair of briefs and was about to pull them on when he felt Nicolai's hand touch his arm. Looking at his lover, Brian saw him shake his head before motioning him toward the bed. The cool breeze from the open window cooled his skin as Nicolai guided him into bed before joining him and pulling the sheet over both of them.

Brian knew they should just go to sleep with Zoe in the next room, and he willed his arousal away, but both his body and Nicolai would have none of it. Rolling him onto his back, Nicolai climbed on top of him, the skin-to-skin contact almost enough to make Brian come right then.

"You handle everything for everyone," Nicolai told him. "People rely on you. Zoe does, I do. Even Dieter and Gerald rely on you. You are always strong for everyone. Tonight let it go." Brian opened his mouth, but felt Nicolai's fingers touch his lips, and whatever he was going to say slipped from his mind. "No sound, just feel," Nicolai said, and then he kissed him, hard, like he was claiming complete and total ownership.

As they kissed, Brian attempted to roll them on the mattress. Nicolai stopped him by breaking the kiss and glaring at him.

Without argument, Brian settled back on the bed, and Nicolai kissed him again before beginning a slow slither down Brian's body.

The sensual skin-on-skin friction sent chills up Brian's spine and made his dick throb between them. Then, to Brian's surprise, Nicolai pushed back the covers and got out of bed. Brian stifled a groan as he watched Nicolai turn out the light and then return to the bed. Brian could see very little. The bed dipped, and then Nicolai's skin pressed to Brian's once again. Nicolai's lips found his in the dark. Brian quivered when he felt Nicolai's hot tongue blaze a trail down his chin before lightly skimming over the skin of his throat.

Brian wondered what Nicolai was going to do next and then felt lips clamp around one of his nipples. He swallowed a small cry as Nicolai licked and sucked his skin. Nicolai kissed meandering trails over Brian's skin, hands caressing him in the wake of his kisses. Brian knew he was being teased, and he had no idea how much more he would be able to take. His dick throbbed and pulsed with every touch, begging for Nicolai's attention.

He tried to hold back the sigh, but couldn't when Nicolai finally took his length in hand, stroking slowly and gently. Brian wanted to beg for more, thrusting his hips into the sensation. Nicolai's hand settled on his hip to still him, and then he was taken to heaven as hot lips surrounded him, sucking hard. In contrast to Nicolai's hands, his lips were ravenous and demanding as they sucked and pulled on his shaft. Brian's legs began to shake as desire and passion warred with the last of Brian's control.

Brian closed his eyes and let the feeling of being loved and cared for wash over him. Clenching the bedding in his fists, Brian knew he had to remain quiet, but all he wanted to do was scream at the top of his lungs as his release built deep inside him. Instead, he clamped his teeth together, eyes crossing, his entire body shaking as he tried to contain and prolong his impending climax. Brian's skin began to tingle, and his head throbbed as he came hard down Nicolai's throat, gasping for breath as waves of indescribable pleasure broke over him.

Brian floated for the longest time, eyes closed, and he really didn't want to come back. Rarely could he remember feeling so boneless and happy, but those times he could were all with Nicolai. Opening his eyes slowly, he saw Nicolai, his amazing lover, staring back at him, a huge smile on his face. Then he was kissed, Nicolai's body clinging to his as Nicolai undulated above him. They continued kissing as Brian hugged Nicolai close, letting his lover take what he needed. Brian heard Nicolai's breath catch, and Nicolai lifted his head, letting Brian see the open-mouthed ecstasy on his face as he came.

Afterward, both of them lay together trying to catch their breath. Eventually, Brian climbed out of bed to get a cloth. After they'd cleaned up, they pulled on briefs and got back into bed.

"Better?" Nicolai asked, and as an answer, Brian took Nicolai's hand in his, bringing it to his lips. Rolling onto his side, Brian felt Nicolai curl next to him, holding him tightly in his arms. "It will be okay," Nicolai said, and then the room was silent, Nicolai's tight embrace telling him all he needed to know. And at least for now, Brian felt as though everything would be okay.

They spent the rest of their week in Austria, having the time of their lives. In the middle of the week, they rented a car and checked out of the hotel, spending the last three days of their vacation touring the country. They toured the fully restored baroque abbey at Melk before driving to Salzburg, where they took a *Sound of Music* tour. Yes, it was touristy, but Zoe had seen the movie and she had a ball. On their last day in Vienna, they saw the Lipizzaner Stallions, and in the evening Brian and Nicolai took Zoe back to the Prater for a few hours while Dieter and Gerald were shown some things in the hotel attic that might have belonged to Dieter's family. A drive through the Alps capped off their vacation in a stunning way before the return to Vienna to catch their flight home.

On the return trip, the five of them were able to sit together, and everyone helped keep Zoe occupied for the long flight home. "Daddy." Zoe lifted her head away from the picture she was coloring looking from Brian to Nicolai and back to Brian. "Is Nicolai going to come live with us?"

Brian didn't know quite what to say to her. "Would that be bad?" Brian asked after his surprise wore off.

"No, Daddy." She gave him one of her eye rolls, as if to say "God, adults are dumb." "You smile when he's around." Zoe returned to her coloring without saying anything more, and Brian looked to the seat next to him, where Nicolai was reading a book, completely oblivious to the conversation that had taken place around him. Brian had thought of repeating his invitation to Nicolai to move in with them, but he knew that as long as Barbara was fighting over Zoe, Nicolai would never do it for fear he'd hurt Brian's case. That was his Nicolai: caring, thoughtful, and concerned about everyone but himself. Reaching across the seat, he lightly touched Nicolai's arm and smiled when he looked his way.

The flight seemed to go on forever, but they finally landed in Chicago. As soon as they were off the plane, the group made their way to the gate for the last leg of their trip, with Dieter and Gerald stopping for Garrett's caramel corn and cheese corn. They spent the entire time they were waiting for the next flight filling Zoe with as much popcorn as she could eat.

"Go wash your hands before we board the plane," Brian told Zoe when she splayed her orange fingers in front of his face before licking the cheesy gunk off her fingers. "Take Uncle Dieter and Uncle Gerald with you. They probably need to wash their hands too."

"No, we don't," Dieter said with a grin after he pulled a fingertip out of his mouth. Wiping his hands on a napkin, Dieter grabbed Zoe, zooming her through the concourse toward the bathrooms, with Gerald following behind. When Brian turned to look at Nicolai, he found him licking cheese off his fingers as well, but Brian knew from the way his pink tongue curled around his fingers that Nicolai was purposely trying to wind him up. It was working, as evidenced by the fact that Brian had to shift things around slightly. Nicolai noticed, grinning slyly as he reached into the bag once again. The others coming back interrupted Nicolai's obvious fun, and with a wink, he headed toward the restrooms. Their flight was called just after Nicolai returned, and they boarded the plane for home. Brian couldn't help wondering as they walked down the Jetway just what was going to greet him when they got home.

CHAPTER 8

LINDA stepped into Brian's office and closed the door. "Your ex-wife is a nutcase," she began before she'd even sat down. "She has no case, and it's obvious that she's only after money. I have witnesses who've heard her say just that. Why is she continuing with this?"

Brian sighed softly. "She's doing it to be spiteful. That's the only possibility. Whenever Zoe stays with her, she comes home and tells me all the bad things her mother said about me. I think the root of all this is money, but I know that Zoe keeps talking about Nicolai, and I bet Barbara has figured out that I'd like to have him move in with us."

"I think you and Nicolai should do it anyway," Linda said.

"Is that my lawyer talking?" Brian asked, and Linda shook her head.

"As your lawyer, I'd tell you you're doing the right thing."

"Not that it matters. Nicolai would never consider moving in as long as this suit is active," Brian explained.

"Have you asked him?" Linda asked, her voice unusually soft.

Brian shook his head. "I don't have to. Nicolai would never do anything that could remotely hurt Zoe. There are times I think he loves her more than her own mother does."

"Then we need to bring this to a head so it doesn't drag on any longer, especially since it affects your daughter," Linda said as she opened her day planner. "It's been almost two months, and that's long enough. And that's why I came to see you. I noticed that you have a few hours this afternoon at four. I asked your ex-wife and her counsel to come in for a meeting, and they agreed."

Brian looked confused. "You asked for the meeting? They must think we're desperate." Brian wasn't sure he liked that.

"That's exactly what I want them to think. We've contacted them, so they'll think we're anxious to settle. Once we get them here, I'll hit them between the eyes."

"What's the plan?" Brian asked, a little intrigued.

Linda shook her head. "Just be at the meeting and agree with whatever I say. I want you to look surprised as well. That way Barbara will know that I'm the instigator rather than you. It'll help give you cover when you deal with her in the future." Linda closed her planner. "On another topic, how's the Supreme Court appeal coming?"

"It's all set except for the oral argument, which is in late September."

"Do you need backup?"

"Gerald is going with me, and I know that Dieter and Nicolai are going as well. They'd both kill us if we tried to leave them home. Besides, I'd be interested to see what Nicolai makes of the justices. He was spot-on in his ability to read the appellate judges."

"So I heard." Linda stood up, tall and almost regal in her bearing. Linda was a pit bull and she wasn't above using her looks if she thought it could give her an advantage. Brian had once seen her show up at a negotiating session in a red dress that had the opposing attorney and the client gaping at her the entire time. She'd walked out of the session with everything she wanted and then immediately went to her office to change clothes.

"He sees things others don't. He may not be able to hear, but he doesn't miss much," Brian explained as he stood up and thanked Linda before she turned to leave. "I'll see you at four." Linda left his office, and Brian went back to work. He wasn't too sure about this meeting, but he trusted Linda and hoped maybe this would be over soon.

At three thirty, Brian's cell buzzed. Pulling it out of his pocket, he saw a message from Nicolai.

> *How late do you need to work? I have*
> *something I'd like to show you.*

Brian typed his message in the tiny keyboard:

> *I have a meeting with Barbara at four.*
> *Depending on how it goes, I could be home at*
> *six or so. Can I let you know?*

Brian sent the message and only waited a minute for the response.

> *Yes. Thinking good thoughts. Tell Linda to let*
> *her have it.*

> *I'll message you when I know.* Brian pressed send.

> *Okay, love you.*

> *Love you too.*

Brian sent the last message with a smile on his face. There were days when he could barely believe that Nicolai loved him or that he'd gotten so lucky, and having Nicolai in his life was really lucky. How many gay men, or anyone for that matter, meet just the right person at just the right time in their life? Not many, so Brian considered himself a very fortunate person.

"Are you ready? Reception just called, and they're here and waiting," Linda said, and Brian closed the file he'd been working on before getting up and heading to the conference room with Linda. Once in the room, she phoned reception and had their opponents brought back.

Barbara looked tired when she walked into the conference room, and her attorney looked to have more in common with a weasel than a human being. Brian wondered which rock he had crawled out from under. Introductions were made, and then Brian took a chair next to Linda, letting her do the talking.

"You asked for this meeting," the ferret lawyer said, and Brian could see he thought he had the upper hand.

"Yes, we did. This has gone on long enough, and the only one being hurt by this action is Zoe. So I was hoping we could sit down and work this out," Linda began. "Because I have to tell you, your case is going nowhere with a judge."

"I'm her mother," Barbara said.

"That means nothing. The courts decide based upon what's best for the child, and over the last decade the bias toward the mother has largely disappeared. The thing is, I figured we could work some things out." Linda opened the file in front of her. "I hired a private investigator to look into a number of things. These include how you spend your time and where you go. It seems you've had a number of people to your residence." Linda began dropping photographs onto the table. "It seems you have what your daughter describes as a lot of 'sleepovers.' I showed these photographs to Zoe, and she identified a number of these men. Do you want me to go on? I certainly can. You spend most of your evenings at a bar called My Office where you seem to be quite popular." Linda dropped another photograph on the table. "These are all certified, and the investigator will testify in court about these and other things he witnessed."

Barbara glared across the table at Brian. "You had me followed?"

Linda cut in. "No, I did. He authorized me to do what was necessary to protect Zoe. She's an amazing child, and she deserves someone who'll take proper care of her." Linda reached into the file again. "I also have records on your history with Zoe. Broken appointments, returning her home late or early without calling… do you want me to go on?"

"He's gay," Barbara cried, her voice filled with desperation. "Has he told you that? He actually has a boyfriend. They took Zoe to Europe, and she said she stayed in the same room with them."

"Actually, they stayed in a suite, and Zoe had her own room," Linda said calmly before producing some of the photographs they'd taken on their trip. Brian had to admit, Linda was damned good. "And for the record, Brian's sexual orientation is not legally pertinent. You may have a problem with your ex-husband's sexual orientation, but the law doesn't." Linda turned to look at the ferret. "So, you brought this suit, what is it you really want?"

Barbara opened her mouth, but her attorney stopped her. "I think we've heard enough for today. We'll see you in court."

"No," Barbara cried, "he's a fag, and I won't have my daughter living with a couple of perverts. I want custody of Zoe right now, and I want him to pay child support."

"That isn't going to happen," Linda said confidently from her chair. "Because we are countersuing, claiming that you are an unfit mother, and if you want visitation, we'll agree as long as it's supervised with the cost of that supervision to come from your remaining alimony payments. I have already contacted child services, and they are ready to make that recommendation as well. So I suggest you sit down." Linda's voice became harsh, and Brian almost jumped at the tone. He'd heard her use it before, and quite frankly, he was just glad she was on his side.

Both Barbara and her attorney sat down, and Barbara leaned over to him. Brian and Linda let them whisper back and forth for a while, and then the attorney turned to Linda. "My client isn't able to live on what she's being paid. She doesn't have another source of income right now. She's looking for a job, but hasn't found anything yet."

Linda looked at Brian and then back at the attorney. Without looking, Linda pulled some papers out of the file. "I know for a fact that she hasn't looked for a job or even typed a résumé. My investigator was very thorough within the limits of the law. And I have it in Barbara's own words." Linda slid some printouts across the table. Brian hadn't seen them, and he wondered just what they were. "My investigator read her blog and had seen all her posts for months. These are perfectly admissible. And I have multiple witnesses. So would you like to try again?"

Brian leaned over to Linda. "I located a career counselor to work with her so she can find a job."

Linda nodded and returned her focus on the pair across from them. "First, before we go any further, I want this suit dropped. We will discuss nothing until you agree to that."

They talked back and forth. "Agreed. The paperwork will be filed today," the ferret lawyer said, and Linda slid more papers across the table.

"These are to be signed before you leave this office. They are the papers you need to withdraw the suit. As I said, nothing will be discussed until that is done." Linda sat back and waited for them to talk before Barbara took a pen from the center of the table. "Just a moment, please." Linda picked up the phone, and one of the legal secretaries entered the conference room. "Margaret will witness your signature and notarize it," Linda explained, and Barbara signed the form. Margaret did as well before sealing and notarizing it.

"I'll make copies and have the originals sent over to the court today," Margaret said before leaving the room. She returned a few minutes later with the copies and then quietly closed the door behind herself.

"Okay. Here's what we will do. Brian has agreed to pay for career counseling, and that offer still stands. He will also add an additional three months onto Barbara's alimony schedule at the current rate, so instead of six months, she'll have nine months. That is all. Her visitation will be every other weekend as it stands in the current custody agreement. However, she is to understand that all the information we have will remain in our custody. There is to be no harassment of my client, and your client is to behave properly toward him and his partner. Brian has been gracious enough not to talk about Barbara's behavior with Zoe and has not said anything derogatory about her. We expect you to extend the same courtesy. Zoe is not a battleground."

Barbara got up to leave and stopped short, turning around. "You really haven't said anything to Zoe?"

"No. Your daughter loves you, and that's important to her. It would hurt her to know how you've behaved, and I try very hard not to let Zoe be hurt. I suggest you do the same," Brian said, keeping the malice out of his voice. Barbara left the room, followed by her attorney, and Brian let out a sigh of relief. "Thank you, Linda, you were brilliant." He knew that at least some of what Linda had said was a bluff. For one thing, Zoe had never been shown any pictures of men, but they didn't need to know that.

"You're welcome. You pointed us in many of the directions. Barbara did the rest." Linda put the papers and pictures back in her file. "Now, when am I going to get an invitation to dinner?" After he'd gotten back from Vienna, Brian had thanked Linda for helping him, and they'd agreed to a fee of one home-cooked meal. Nicolai had agreed to do the cooking, and it was now time for the two of them to pay up.

"I'll talk to Nicolai tomorrow, and we'll set a date. Nicolai is a fantastic cook, and he does better in small groups, so it'll just be the four of us, unless you'd like to bring a date."

"No. A small, quiet dinner sounds wonderful." Linda left the conference room, and Brian breathed a sigh of relief like he could never remember. Fishing out his phone, Brian sent Nicolai a text that he was getting ready to leave the office. Nicolai replied, asking him to come to his house.

Back in his office, Brian packed up and sent Nicolai a text with his acceptance before stopping at his admin's desk and leaving her a note to send Linda her favorite flowers. Then he hurried toward the exit and down to his car. Brian felt as though he was as light as air. A huge weight had been lifted from his shoulders, and at the same time a whole new set of possibilities for a life with Nicolai was opening in front of him. However, as he got in his car, a whole new set of concerns began to take root. What if Nicolai said no? Brian had already asked him once to move in with him, and he'd turned him down because of concerns over Zoe and how that might affect her, but what if that was just an excuse? Brian knew he was hopelessly in love with his Nicolai, and he wanted to be with him all the time. Brian also knew that Nicolai was an independent person, and maybe he would want to maintain that independence. He'd worked hard to get over and break away from Justin, so maybe he didn't want to go through the possibility of another relationship like that again.

A ton of possibilities raced through Brian's mind, and he tried his best to keep them a bay as he drove to Nicolai's house. Neither of them had broached the subject of moving in together with Barbara's lawsuit hanging over their heads, and now Brian was both excited and nervous as he prepared to ask the big question once again. They communicated in various ways about so many other things, so why was this subject so hard? As soon as he asked himself the question, he knew the answer: because it was so important, and because Brian wanted this so badly. Pulling up in front of Nicolai's house, it looked dark, and Brian sent Nicolai a text that he was out front and then waited.

I'm in the garage was the response, so Brian got out, walking around the side of the house to the large garage in back. Nicolai had converted two of the bays into a glass workshop and studio, while the third bay was still used for his car. Opening the door, Brian peered inside. Nicolai was bent over a table, piecing together what looked like part of a broken stained-glass window. When Nicolai looked up, he smiled, and Brian stepped inside, closing the door behind him. "How did it go?" Nicolai signed after gently setting down the piece of glass he'd been holding.

"Linda was amazing, and Barbara dropped the suit. In exchange, we agreed to extend her alimony a few months," Brian signed back. He and Zoe still went to sign language class two days a week and both of them were getting better. When it was just the two of them, Brian tried to sign as much as he could so he could reinforce his lessons, and he was surprised how easily new concepts came once he'd learned the basics. He still reverted to spelling new words or phrases, and Nicolai would then supply the proper sign.

"So there's no chance of you losing Zoe?" Nicolai asked, moving closer to him.

"No. We had things on Barbara that she couldn't deny, and she realized it was hopeless," Brian answered, smiling when Nicolai moved into his outstretched arms once he'd finished signing. Hugging Nicolai for a while, Brian basked in their shared happiness and the feel of his lover in his arms. After a while, Nicolai backed away, looking into his eyes.

"I have something to show you. Something special," Nicolai signed, and then he motioned toward the window on the table. "I got this a few days ago. I was driving and saw it at a yard sale. It has some broken glass, but I can fix that. If you like it, I thought we could mount it in a frame with a light behind it for your living room." Nicolai was so excited, his hands flew as he made the signs, and Brian had to pay close attention so he didn't miss anything.

"It's beautiful," he signed, looking at the window. Even lying on the table, Brian could tell it was extraordinary. It would be spectacular with light shining through it.

"It's missing some of the panes of glass that make up the sky, but there is enough remaining that I can fabricate the missing pieces. I've studied his work, and I know the techniques they used to make this particular type of glass."

"I'd love to have it in the living room. It's beautiful, but what has you so excited?"

"Brian," Nicolai spoke, "this is a Tiffany Tree of Life window. It's an amazing find, and when I'm done, no one will be able to tell it was ever damaged."

"Thank you, I think it will look amazing in our living room," Brian signed, emphasizing the word "our," and paused to let the message sink in. "I asked you to move in with me before, and I'm doing it again. Only this time I'm asking you the way I should have before. Nicolai, I want you with me all the time. I want to ask you to be my partner, live with me, and help me build a family."

"What about Zoe? Have you asked her about this?"

"I have spoken with her, and she said that you made me smile. You don't have to decide today, but I wanted you to know how I felt and that I love you so very much." Brian had given up trying to sign and made sure Nicolai could see his face.

Nicolai stared at him for a few seconds and then leapt into Brian's arms, hugging him so tight he could barely breathe.

"I love you so much," Brian said again, forgetting in his excitement that Nicolai couldn't hear him. "Does this mean yes?" Brian asked when Nicolai looked into his eyes. Nicolai nodded and then kissed him. Brian got all the information he needed from the way Nicolai's lips attacked his. Brian's cock got instantly hard, and he felt Nicolai's shaft pressing against his as they held each other. Breaking the kiss, Brian looked around the studio, but then stopped himself. There was no way they were going to celebrate a decision to become partners and build a family together by rutting around on the floor of Nicolai's studio. Nicolai was special, and Brian was damned well going to show him just how special he was. "Would you pack a bag and come home with me?"

"Yes," Nicolai answered. "I have to clean up here first."

Brian helped Nicolai as best he could, and after locking and setting the alarm on the glass studio, they walked to Nicolai's house, and Brian waited while he packed a bag. They had a lot to talk about, but Brian knew they would work out the details so things worked for both of them. Once he came downstairs, Nicolai explained that he needed his own car, so they agreed to meet back at Brian's house. Driving as fast as he could, Brian hurried home.

"Hi, Daddy," Zoe called from the living room when he entered the house. For once, she and Aunt Georgia weren't upstairs playing video games.

"Hey, Brian," Georgia called, already shrugging into her jacket. "I have a study date and need to get going."

"Is that what they're calling it now?" Brian quipped, and she flipped him the bird from behind Zoe's back. "Then I'm right," Brian said with a smile. "Have fun." Reaching into his wallet, he handed her some money, and she thanked him before hurrying out of the house with an excited grin on her face.

"I have something I need to tell you," Brian said as he sat on the sofa next to where Zoe had been reading. "Nicolai is going to come live with us. Is that okay with you? I know this may be hard for you to understand, but I love him."

"Daddy, I know about these things." This time she rolled her whole head as well as her eyes. "Sheesh."

"You know I'll never stop loving you, right?" Brian pulled his daughter into a tight hug as he heard the front door open. "I love you very much," Brian said, kissing his daughter's hair.

"I love you too, Daddy," Zoe said before hugging him back. There were very few things in this world that Brian loved as much as his daughter and one of them very possibly just walked through the door. Brian heard Nicolai climb the stairs, and he knew he was giving them some time alone. "Is Nicolai going to love me like you do?" Zoe asked.

"No one will ever love you like I do, but he loves you very much," Brian told her before giving Zoe another hug. "Do you have anything you want to ask?" Zoe shook her head. "If you do, you know you can ask." Brian stood up, and Zoe put her book aside before hurrying upstairs. Brian followed to see what Nicolai was up to, but Zoe beat him to it and was already challenging Nicolai to the races.

Brian let them play and pulled out his phone to order takeout for dinner. He was about to call when he heard the doorbell. Shoving the phone back in his pocket, Brian descended the stairs. Opening the door, he was a bit surprised to see his mother. "How are you?" Brian asked as she stepped inside.

"I'm fine," she answered as she took the dish she carried into the kitchen. "I figured you and Zoe had been eating nothing but pizza and thought you could use some home cooking."

Brian peered under the lid, and his stomach growled at the smell of his mother's baked ziti. "Thank you, Mom," Brian said before turning on the oven and opening the door so his mom could slide the dish inside. Closing the oven door, Brian leaned back against the counter. "I have something to tell you, and I'm not sure how you're going to feel about it." His mother looked at him warily. "Nicolai and I are…." Brian faltered, not quite able to find the right words. He found it ironic that he made his living with words, but couldn't find the right ones for his mother. "Nicolai and I have decided to live together."

"I'm happy for you, dear," she said with a smile that looked surprisingly genuine. Even though his mother had come a long way, he was surprised she was taking this so well. "Don't look at me that way. I found this group, and they helped me realize that I need to be supportive. They've answered so many of my questions. They're mothers and fathers just like me, with gay children. It's called PFLAG, and they were really very nice."

Zoe bounded down the stairs. "Grandma," she cried before reaching for a hug. "Nicolai is going to be living here with us," Zoe told her excitedly. After exchanging hugs, Zoe bounded back up the stairs.

"Are you going to stay to eat with us?"

"No, I have to get back home, but I didn't want you to starve or get fat from all that junk food you eat." His mother patted his belly before leaving. Brian watched her go and then climbed the stairs.

"Zoe, your grandma brought dinner, so go get washed up." Zoe nodded and turned off the game, hurrying to the bathroom. Nicolai looked a bit confused, so Brian signed what had happened, and together they went downstairs. Nicolai helped him set the table, and when Zoe joined them, they all sat down to eat. Afterward, Brian and Nicolai cleaned up while Zoe finished her homework.

At bedtime, Zoe hugged both of them good night before getting cleaned up. Brian made sure she was tucked in. "I'm glad Nicolai is here. He's special."

"So are you," Brian told her with a small lump in his throat. "I'll see you in the morning." Brian kissed her good night before turning off the lights and leaving the room.

He and Nicolai went to bed an hour or so later, where they celebrated their new commitment to one another. Deep, quietly sensual lovemaking stole their breath away as they physically expressed a commitment to each other that words seemed inadequate to describe. Their hands caressed and stroked warm skin as their hearts reached out to each other. Lips kissed as their souls formed those first permanent connections that would bind them together and make both of them feel incomplete without the other. Joining physically, they became one in a way that stayed with them after their earth-shattering releases. Afterward, as they held each other in the dark, Brian listened to the soft sound of Nicolai's breathing, realizing that now all he had to do was finish the task that had brought them together in the first place.

CHAPTER 9

DIETER saw him in the lobby of the National Hotel in Washington, DC, and he rushed over to where Nicolai was sitting, taking the chair next to his. "Tomorrow's the big day," Dieter said, clearly nervous, "the Supreme Court."

"Yes. But Brian told me it could be months before they publish their decision," Nicolai explained, trying to get his friend to calm down a little. Dieter looked about ready to jump completely out of his skin.

"I know—I just can't help it. You saw me at the appellate hearing. I was a nervous wreck then, and I feel just as churned up now."

Nicolai smiled. "Didn't Gerald help you relax?" Nicolai said with a wink. When Dieter blushed bright red, Nicolai knew he'd done just that. Too bad there wasn't time for Gerald to try again, because it sure looked to Nicolai like Dieter could use it.

"How are things with you and Brian? Have you decided what you're going to do with your house yet?" Nicolai shook his head, and he saw Dieter's eyebrows lift before he shifted in his chair. "You haven't moved out yet, have you? You're still keeping your house. Why?"

"I need my studio," Nicolai explained easily. He'd been telling himself the same thing for the past two months, but he was lying to Dieter, just like he'd been lying to himself.

"That's bull. Brian would build you a studio. In fact, he asked me to help him figure out what you'd need as a surprise, and if you tell him I blabbed, I'll never forgive you." Now it was Nicolai's turn to be surprised. "He loves you so much."

"I know he does, but so did Justin, and look what happened with him." Finally Nicolai admitted a little of what he'd been afraid of.

"Brian isn't Justin, and you know it."

"You never knew Justin," Nicolai countered.

"No, I didn't," Nicolai saw Dieter say. "But I know that Brian would never treat you the way Justin did. Brian would never dump you like Justin did, and he'd certainly treat you better. I know you love Brian. I can see it in the way you look at him, and he loves you. Probably the only person in the world he loves more is Zoe, and that's different because she's his daughter. So what's really holding you back?"

Nicolai processed what Dieter said before shrugging his shoulders. He wished he could put his finger on exactly what it was that scared him. "I worked very hard to become independent after Justin left," Nicolai said, trying to explain some of what he was feeling. "I don't want to go through that again."

Dieter shook his head slightly. "How much time are you actually spending at your house? You aren't." Dieter answered his own question before Nicolai could stop him. "You're at Brian's every night, and most of your things are at Brian's. I know it's hard, but you're paying for a house you don't use just because you're afraid Brian will turn out like Justin." Dieter shook his head. "If Justin were here, I'd punch him out good." Dieter looked as fierce as Nicolai had ever seen him. When Dieter stood up, Nicolai followed his gaze and saw Brian and Gerald walking toward them. Brian extended his hand and helped Nicolai to his feet. Together, the four of them walked across the National Mall to their destination.

Nicolai tried with all his might to keep his nerves in check as he followed Brian up the steps of the Supreme Court building in Washington, DC. Dieter was right behind him, and Nicolai could feel the nervous energy radiating off him in waves. This was it. The court would decide if Dieter would get his family legacy back. Well, that wasn't totally true. It was all a muddle to him, but Brian explained that the court would most likely rule on the question of whether Dieter could sue for the return of his family's paintings in US courts. It really was a bit confusing, but Nicolai knew that winning meant a huge boost in Dieter's favor and increased the likelihood that he'd get the five Pirktl paintings, his family legacy, returned.

They had flown into Washington the day before and overnighted at an amazing hotel. Zoe was staying with her grandmother, but Nicolai found he already missed her.

Dieter stopped in the middle of the stairs and turned to look back toward the Capitol. Nicolai stopped, too, as did both Gerald and Brian. Nicolai saw Dieter swallow and then sigh. "I knew this was going to be a long journey, and I can hardly believe that we're here." Dieter held out his hands, and they all added theirs, clasping hands in a group handshake. "I could not have done this without all of you. Gerald, you believed in me and figured out how to make this happen in the first place. Brian, you supported us through the trial, saw us through the appeal, and became one of the best friends I've ever had." Nicolai saw Dieter begin to choke up. "And Nicolai...." Dieter paused, and Nicolai knew Dieter was searching for something to say. He knew that both Gerald and Brian had worked very hard to help return Dieter's family legacy, but he really hadn't done anything. There had been many times while they were planning this trip that he'd wondered why he was even going along. "You're my brother in every way except blood. When I was a child, I wanted a brother very badly. I didn't get one then, but I have one now,"

Nicolai saw Dieter say, and then he was pulled into a hug, feeling very close to tears.

Dieter stepped back so Nicolai could see his face. "Now let's go win this thing."

They walked the rest of the way up the steps before showing their identification and then passing through metal detectors as Gerald's and Brian's bags were passed through X-ray machines. They emerged on the other side and were directed to the actual courtroom, where a long, polished bench with nine chairs sat on a slightly raised dais. Gerald and Brian took their places at the table for the plaintiffs while Nicolai sat next to Dieter in one of the gallery benches. There were a few other people in attendance, but Nicolai ignored them. Taking Dieter's hand, he tried to calm him. It didn't work, and Dieter continued to fidget, jumping slightly at every sound. Nicolai's excitement built to the point that he nearly forgot that it wasn't even his case that was being heard. Nicolai had seen Dieter's reaction in the museum, and he'd worried for months how his friend would fare if he lost. Regardless of what Dieter might say, Nicolai knew his friend was hanging a lot on the return of the paintings and would be devastated if the court ruled against them.

Nicolai felt Dieter tense and saw him turn his head, and Nicolai followed his gaze, recognizing the opposing attorney from the appeal. He and his colleague took their places, and a few minutes later, a man rose and everyone followed. Then Nicolai watched as several people in black robes with solemn looks on their faces filed into the courtroom from different doors. Nicolai felt a bit awed as the nine justices of the Supreme Court took their places. Once they were seated, everyone else sat, and Nicolai saw what had to be the chief justice call the court to order. After he spoke for a while, Nicolai saw address Brian directly.

The sense of pride that filled Nicolai as he saw Brian standing confidently in front of the highest court in the land took him by surprise. Brian stood tall, and to Nicolai's eyes, exuded self-assurance. Nicolai knew in his heart that what Brian was arguing was right and on the side of justice, and he knew Brian knew it too. After Brian spoke for about five minutes, he was interrupted by one of the justices with what looked like a question.

From where he sat, he could see Brian answer the question, but couldn't tell what his answer was. Instead, Nicolai did what he'd done at the appeal hearing and watched the justices. They all seemed engaged and listening, but as Brian answered the questions, he saw some of the anxiety present in a few of the justices abate slightly. He wasn't sure what it meant, but he continued to watch as the justices went on asking questions. A few times, they turned to opposing counsel for a brief rebuttal. Brian looked magnificent as he handled whatever the justices threw at him. He could see the smallest signs of tension in Brian, but only because he knew exactly what to look for. To the rest of the world, he looked totally in control, and that was as sexy as hell.

Some of the justices seemed to take turns asking questions, and then to Nicolai's relief, Brian sat down. Nicolai saw him turn and wink at him before returning his attention to the justices. The chief justice spoke again, and then the opposing attorney got his turn. This time, the questioning seemed livelier, at least to Nicolai. After some length of time, Nicolai saw the questioning stop. Then everyone rose, and the justices left the chamber.

Once they were gone and the door closed behind them, Brian and Gerald got up and met Dieter and Nicolai on their way out. Nicolai couldn't tell if anyone was speaking, but if they were, he didn't see it. "Is that it?" Dieter asked, turning toward him as he spoke.

"Yes," Brian answered, signing as he did for Nicolai's benefit. "What did you think? Did you get any feel from them?" Brian asked him with an excited smile.

"Can we go back to the hotel?"

"Yes," Brian signed, and they left the building, descending the imposing stairs in front of the building before walking across the

Capitol complex and the Mall to the hotel. It was not quite noon, but they headed into the hotel bar, regardless, because it was nearly empty.

Nicolai took a seat and Brian sat next to him, lightly touching his arm. Nicolai gathered his thoughts before speaking. "It looked to me as though at least four were probably with you. Their faces were relaxed, and there was a certain brightness in their eyes when they spoke. The lines around their eyes faded, and when the other side spoke, their eyes closed slightly. There are two that are probably against you—they reacted just the opposite of the other four. The rest I wasn't sure about. Overall, it looked to me as though they accepted what you were saying really well."

"I know, but everyone says you can never tell how the court will rule by the oral argument. Many of the justices like to play devil's advocate, so you never really know what they're thinking," Brian said as he signed for Nicolai.

"You're getting really good at that," Dieter said. "Do you think you could teach me to sign?"

"Brian takes classes at the Institute for the Deaf. You could go with him. They have classes going all the time," Nicolai explained, and the conversation seemed to move away from the hearing for now. Nicolai knew that they'd come back to it again and again over the course of the day.

A server brought them menus from the restaurant, and they ordered lunch. Brian and Gerald began talking about the hearing again with Dieter, while Nicolai let his mind wander. Now that the hearing was over, he let himself relax and watched as his friends talked. Nicolai found his attention drawn to Brian's mouth, thinking of the way it looked when he talked or smiled, the way he tasted when he kissed him, and the amazing things he'd learned to do with it when he was in bed. Then Brian's eyes locked on his, and Nicolai saw the amazing lover and friend he had in his life. Brian continued speaking with Gerald, but Nicolai could see his amazing brown eyes shining at him, filled with love and care. Nicolai had looked into those eyes so many times, felt their intensity and peered into their depths. Brian moved his chair a little closer, and then Nicolai felt his hand on his leg. As he watched his lover, he thought of Dieter's questions and realized he really didn't have a good answer. If Brian, and Zoe for that matter, were each willing to take a chance and let him into their lives, he could certainly do the same thing.

Nicolai had to give Brian a lot of credit. After they'd decided to move in together, Brian hadn't pushed or pressed him. Instead, he'd let Nicolai move at his own pace. Nicolai realized that alone should have been a huge clue as to the type of man Brian was.

"Are you okay?" Brian signed.

"I'm just thinking," Nicolai responded.

"Is it something you'd like to talk about?"

"When we return to the room," Nicolai signed in response to Brian's question, and his lover nodded his acceptance of the answer as the server brought their orders, setting the plates in front of them.

Nicolai didn't even try to keep up with the conversation around the table. It was too much, and if there was anything important, Brian would tell him about it, or he'd bring him into the conversation. Nicolai cut a bite of his beef, stopping the bite halfway to his mouth as he had one of those "I'm such an idiot" moments. He trusted Brian enough to tell him if there was something important he needed to know. As far as Nicolai knew, Brian had never kept anything from him and had always been honest and forthright with him. Dieter was right—it was time for him to move on, and Brian most certainly wasn't Justin. How long was he going to let that asshole have a hold on his life?

"Are you sure you're okay?" Brian signed. "Is the food not good?"

Nicolai set down his fork and looked at the three men around the table before letting his gaze settle on Brian. "Do any of you happen to know a good Realtor?"

Brian looked slightly confused for a second, but smiled as the impact of the question hit home, and Nicolai grinned. Nicolai saw Dieter smile as well, nodding slowly. Nicolai felt pretty happy himself, like he'd settled something that had been keeping him at loose ends for a long time. As he finished his lunch, Nicolai kept looking at Brian, who, he noticed, kept looking back at him as well.

Once they finished eating, Brian signed the check. Neither Dieter nor Nicolai had been to Washington, DC, before, and since they weren't scheduled to leave until the following day, they decided to take in some of the sights. The afternoon was spent looking at rockets and airplanes in the Air and Space Museum as well as wandering around the Mall to look at the memorials. After dark, they walked to the Lincoln Memorial and stood on the steps, looking at the seated Lincoln with the entire building bathed in light.

"We're walking to see the Jefferson Memorial—do you want to come along?" Nicolai saw Dieter ask.

Nicolai looked at Brian and saw him his shake his head. "I think we're heading back to the hotel. We'll meet you in the lobby in the morning," Brian explained as he signed for Nicolai's benefit.

Brian took his hand, and they crossed the street and slowly walked along the path that wound under the trees next to the reflecting pools. At the World War II Memorial, they stopped and watched the fountains before continuing along the lighted paths, the cool night breeze rustling the leaves over their heads and causing a shower of yellow, brown, and red leaves on the path ahead. They didn't talk at all. If they needed to communicate, they used their eyes and small gestures that conveyed so much.

Nicolai was in love, completely and totally. He'd been that way for a long time, but now he felt free and light. Leaning close to Brian, he smiled up at his lover, and in a small copse of trees, Brian kissed him with an energy Nicolai had never felt before. The kiss almost seemed electric, and Nicolai felt the hair on the back of his neck stand on end and he was instantly aroused, a leg quivering with anticipation. They'd kissed many times, but for some reason this felt so different, like the last of Nicolai's reservations had fallen away. Brian's lips tasted different, sweeter, and the touch of his hand on his arm slightly warmer and tingly. After breaking the kiss, Brian looked into Nicolai's eyes, and he shivered despite his warm jacket, but it wasn't from the cold.

In the lobby of their hotel, Brian didn't release his hand as they walked toward the elevators. Nicolai saw people look at them, but Brian paid them no mind as he pushed the call button. When the doors slid open, they stepped inside and rode to their floor, still hand in hand. As the car rose, Nicolai's excitement built, and he could feel the energy flowing from Brian, like something powerful was lurking inside him that needed to be let loose.

Brian opened the hotel-room door, and Nicolai stepped inside. Once the door closed, Brian tugged him into his arms, kissing him hard. Brian had always been a considerate, careful lover, but tonight something felt different, more energetic, and Nicolai liked it.

Brian backed him toward the bed, and Nicolai put himself in Brian's hands. His legs bumped the edge of the mattress, and Brian kissed him down onto it. Then, to Nicolai's dismay, Brian stepped away again. When Nicolai moved toward him, Brian held up a finger for him to stop.

With almost painful slowness, Brian began opening the buttons of his shirt, and Nicolai shifted on the bed when he saw Brian's honey-colored skin. He loved the look of this man, *his* man, and Nicolai automatically opened his jacket, dropping it on the floor. When Nicolai reached to pull off his shirt, Brian shook his head before locking their eyes together. Nicolai let his hands fall to his sides.

Brian pulled open his shirt, shrugging it off his shoulders before draping the fabric over a chair. Brian then toed off his shoes before pulling off his belt and opening his pants, turning around and giving Nicolai a great view of his backside. Nicolai's mouth went dry as Brian stepped out of his pants, and Nicolai hoped the briefs would be next, but that wasn't to be, at least not right now.

Brian stalked toward the bed, his hips swaying slightly. Nicolai swallowed, wondering what Brian was going to do next. His lover's hands gripped his knees and then slowly slid along his thighs. Nicolai let his head drop back, and when Brian's hand stroked along his jeans-covered length, he felt his breath hitch. Brian had told him he made lots of sounds when they made love, and Nicolai wasn't sure whether he was making any now, but he sort of felt like he was. He thought he had to be. What Brian was doing to him felt too good to keep buried inside. Nicolai thrust his hips forward, wishing he could get out of his pants. He shifted on the bed as if his body was trying to leave his pants behind.

Finally, Nicolai felt Brian's hand on the hem of his shirt and he sat up, lifting his arms so Brian could tug the shirt off. The room was a little cool, and the air kissed his skin, raising small goose bumps and making his nipples hard even before Brian's tongue circled them. Brian pressed him back onto the mattress as Nicolai felt his skin being devoured. Brian licked and kissed him everywhere, his lover's mouth refusing to settle. "Want you," Nicolai said, hoping he was somewhat coherent.

"I want you too," he read on Brian's lips just before he was kissed within an inch of his life. Brian's fingers worked open first his belt and then the catch on his pants. The fabric parted, and Nicolai raised his hips as a silent request for Brian to remove them. He didn't. Instead, he lifted Nicolai's legs, repositioning him on the bed before kissing him possessively. "I love you, Nicolai, and you're mine and I'm yours." Nicolai saw him accentuate the words.

"What brought this on?" Nicolai signed, not that he was really complaining, but he wanted to know, so he could do it again.

Brian sat back on his legs, his hands resting on Nicolai's chest, the hyperawareness of the touch working deep into Nicolai's body. "I waited two months after you said you would be my partner for you to actually let go and trust that I love you, and today you did that. I want you to know that you are mine and you will always be mine, and I will always be yours." Brian lifted his hands off Nicolai's chest, their heat fading away. "Nothing is going to change that," Brian signed. "Do you understand?"

"Yes," Nicolai signed. "I'm sorry it took so long."

"Don't be sorry, just be mine forever," Brian signed back.

"Yes," Nicolai said, and Brian kissed him, cutting off further conversation, which was just fine. Nicolai had always thought mouth-talking was overrated—it was much better to use your mouth for something more productive. And Brian did just that.

Brian kept an arm across the top of his chest, so Nicolai was unable to see, only feel. And when Brian's fingers worked their way beneath the waistband of his briefs, Nicolai stilled, the anticipation nearly killing him. Brian drew his cock out of his underwear, leaving the band pressing just below his balls. For a second, Nicolai felt silly hanging out like this. That was, until he felt Brian's warm breath across his skin. Nicolai tensed, and his cock jumped and throbbed. Brian's fingers wound tightly around the base, and he felt Brian's tongue slide around the head, but go no further.

Nicolai stretched as tightly as he could, arching his back, nearly his entire body coming off the bed as he forced his body into a bridge, trying as hard as he could to get Brian to give him more. Releasing his breath, Nicolai collapsed back onto the bed, and then Brian took him deep. Nicolai shuddered from head to toe as Brian worked him hard, letting him move his hips back and forth. It didn't take long before Nicolai felt the first tingles beginning at the base of his spine. Thrusting for more, his eyes opened wide as Brian's lips slid away. He probably said something, but Nicolai didn't know what. Nicolai felt his shoes slip off his feet and then his pants were yanked down his legs, followed by his underwear. Before he knew what was happening, Brian had flipped him on the bed and hot, searing lips kissed their way down his back, hands caressing his cheeks before spreading them wide.

Nicolai arched his back when he felt Brian's tongue slide over his opening. That felt so damned unbelievably hot that Nicolai could barely catch his breath. Fingers teased his skin while Brian's tongue seared his flesh. Pressing back, he pushed into the sensation, and Brian pushed deeper into his body.

Brian kept licking and sucking on his skin as Nicolai felt a finger slowly slide into his body, pull out, and then slide in once again. Nicolai swallowed around the breath that tried to whoosh from his body, and he wasn't sure if he wanted to slide away or press back for more. By the time Brian added a second finger, he'd settled on pressing back for more. His cock throbbed against the bed, and he could feel the slight stickiness on his belly. With every movement, his dick slid against the sheets, and Nicolai was well on his way to climax when Brian's fingers slid away. The bed rocked, and Brian took him by the hips, lifting them off the bed, leaving his butt in the air. A hand continually caressed his butt while he waited. Then a slick finger slid into him, followed by another, before withdrawing again.

Nicolai braced for what was to come and felt Brian's chest against his back as his lover slowly entered his body. The care Brian took with him nearly blew Nicolai's mind. Up to now, Brian had been reticent about taking the active role in their lovemaking, but he seemed to be making up for that now. With near maddening care, Brian continued to deepen their connection until Nicolai felt Brian's hips snug against his butt, and then he stopped and waited a frustratingly long time before slowly beginning to move.

Brian played his body like an instrument, but Nicolai felt separated from his lover even as Brian was deep inside his body. When most couples made love in this position, their voices kept them connected, but Nicolai simply felt alone. At first, when Brian pulled out of him, Nicolai wondered what was happening, but then Brian tapped his hip and helped him roll onto his back. Instantly, Nicolai looked into Brian's eyes and felt a connection to his lover. Lifting his legs, Nicolai's eyes drifted closed when Brian filled him once again, only to have them fly open when Brian hit that spot inside him.

Nicolai gripped the bed as wave after wave of pleasure washed over him. Sweat broke out on Brian's skin, which made him look a little like a glistening gladiator fresh from the arena, and Nicolai loved that fantasy. Pulling his gladiator toward him, Nicolai kissed Brian hard as Brian's cock brushed over that spot inside him again and again. Brian had brought him to the brink more than once, and he wasn't sure how long he was going to last now. When Brian straightened up and gripped him tight, Nicolai lost it, his entire body shaking as he came in a blinding rush that left him breathless, and the room went dark for a few seconds.

The next thing he remembered was Brian stroking his skin. Opening his eyes, he saw Brian's eyes staring back at him, full of concern and worry. Nicolai smiled and stroked Brian's arm before feeling the big cock inside him start to move once more. Nicolai held on and rode the tide of residual pleasure as Brian throbbed inside him and a blissful look shone from his lover's face. Brian was gorgeous when he came, the happiness plain and as beautiful as anything Nicolai had ever seen.

Neither of them moved for a while, savoring the afterglow and the feeling of connection. Nicolai quivered when their bodies separated, and Brian climbed off the bed, returning with a warm cloth. Gently, Brian cleaned his skin before leaning down for a kiss. After drying his skin, Brian climbed onto the bed with him, holding Nicolai tight. They lay together until Brian reached for the phone. Once he'd hung up, Nicolai stretched before looking at Brian.

"That was Gerald. He said they would meet us for dinner in half an hour if we'd like to go," Brian signed, standing naked near the bed. Part of Nicolai didn't want to move and wished Brian would just get back in bed, but his stomach had other ideas. Slowly, Nicolai forced himself out of the bed and began getting dressed. Once he'd pulled on his briefs, Brian's arms wound around his waist, and they stood without moving, Brian's chest pressing to his back. Nicolai leaned back into the touch, content to simply be held for a while. Closing his eyes, Nicolai let the simple act of being held by someone he loved touch his heart. They made love, they kissed, but this simple act of closeness and kindness told him more that all the words in the world.

Turning in Brian's arms, he met his eyes. "You were amazing today, and I was so proud of you. Those judges were intimidating, and you looked strong and confident. It was probably one of the sexiest things I have ever seen, and it made me proud to be your lover and partner."

"Is that what made you decide to sell your house and really come live with me, with us?" Nicolai read on Brian's lips, and saw his eyes display suspicion.

"Yes and no. Seeing you like that made me realize that I was being foolish—that I'd already given my heart to you and that moving in with you was simply geography. And if that's true, then I want my geography to be as close to yours as possible." Nicolai stepped closer, hugging Brian tight, contentment and peace washing over him. He didn't need more words—Brian's touch and closeness were all he needed to tell that his lover felt the same way.

"How long will Dieter have to wait until he gets an answer from the court?" Nicolai asked, stepping away so he could get dressed, but still watching Brian.

"It could be months, but just being here and getting the court to hear our case was a win. Many other countries, and even the United States government, wrote briefs asking the court not to rule in our favor. These briefs do not mean much to the court, but it says that we don't have many people on our side."

"I'm on your side," Nicolai said before turning to get his pants out of his suitcase. A tap on his shoulder stopped him, and Nicolai turned around.

"I know you are, and that is all I'll ever need." Brian kissed him, and Nicolai returned it, letting his pants drop to the floor as he once again lost himself in the best part of his life. Brian was his lover, friend, confidant, and now partner in life. Nicolai didn't need a ceremony or anything else to tell him that. It was in his heart, and that was the only place he needed it.

EPILOGUE

BRIAN opened the door to Nicolai's studio and stepped inside. He could hear Nicolai working in the glass portion of the studio. Instead of building a single studio, they'd ended up building two. Most of the space had been set aside for Nicolai's glass work, but a separate room with great light had been constructed so Nicolai could work on fine art as well. They had added onto the garage, putting in a door directly from the main part of the house. Brian saw Nicolai bent over his work table, carefully fitting the last piece of glass in an exquisite window he'd been working to repair for a local church. Waiting until Nicolai stepped back to check his work, Brian stepped closer, and he knew when Nicolai saw him because of his smile and the way his eyes brightened. To Brian, Nicolai was the most beautiful man in the world, and that particular smile, the one he seemed to reserve only for Brian, was proof, even if very few other people ever saw it.

"Are you about finished?" Brian signed. Over the past six months, since Nicolai had officially moved in after returning from Brian's Supreme Court appearance, he'd become very proficient, and they signed with each other almost exclusively. Neither Nicolai nor his instructors could believe how quickly Brian picked up sign language, but Brian had been motivated, and Nicolai had been a patient and helping partner to both him and Zoe.

"I need ten more minutes and this will be done," Nicolai signed, and Brian nodded, leaning in for a kiss, which he got.

"Ooooh, kissing," he heard someone croon from behind him.

Brian didn't let it stop him, and he took another before turning to his daughter. "Get ready to go," he said as well as signed. It was becoming such a habit that they almost always signed everything among the three of them now. "Uncle Gerald and Uncle Dieter are going to pick us up in half an hour, and you haven't even had your shower yet." Brian gave Nicolai a quick smile before shooing Zoe out of the studio, closing the door behind him. "What are you going to wear?" Brian asked as he climbed the stairs right behind Zoe. He knew he was adding a bit of pressure, but he needed one of them dressed and ready to go.

"It's a surprise," Zoe told him, hurrying to close her bedroom door so he couldn't peek inside.

"Then get cleaned up and ready to go. I'm going to get dressed too, and then Nicolai can get ready."

Zoe hurried toward the bathroom, pausing at the door. "No peeking," she admonished before closing the door. A few minutes later, Brian heard the shower start, and he went into the bedroom. Once he'd closed the door, he hurried to the closet, pulling out his tuxedo before laying it on the bed. Undressing, he began to pull on his clothes for the evening. As he was finishing, the door opened and Nicolai walked in.

"Is Zoe out of the bathroom?" Brian asked, and Nicolai nodded before hurrying into theirs. Brian heard the water start almost right away and wished he had time to join him. Even though it was a Saturday, Nicolai had been working most of the day, so Brian hadn't seen him much. Brian finished dressing before laying Nicolai's clothes on the bed and leaving the room. "Zoe, are you almost dressed?" he asked from outside her door.

"Yes, Dad. I'll be down soon," she answered, and Brian carried his shoes down the stairs with him. Sitting down, he placed his shoes on the floor before peering up at the lighted window that hung on their wall. Nicolai did amazing work, and the scene and colors in the Tiffany window were breathtaking. He could hardly believe Nicolai had given it to him. Turning to another wall, he saw the side-by-side picture hooks where the Dürer woodcuts that Dieter had given them normally hung. After pulling on his shoes, Brian sat back and listened to the sounds from upstairs.

Heavy footsteps on the stairs attracted his attention. Turning, he saw Nicolai step off the bottom step. He looked amazing in his tuxedo, and Brian swallowed, trying to catch his breath. Standing up, Brian hurried into the kitchen, returning with a single white rose boutonniere. After pinning it on Nicolai's lapel, Nicolai kissed him sweetly. "Did you get one for yourself?" Nicolai signed, and Brian shook his head.

"Was Zoe about ready?"

Nicolai smiled conspiratorially. "Yes," he signed.

Brian heard footsteps, relieved that Zoe was on her way. She walked down the stairs, her blue dress shimmering in the light. Brian was speechless. Zoe looked like a young lady, beautiful and stunning. His little girl was growing up. Hurrying to the kitchen, Brian returned with a white rose wrist corsage, placing it on her still-small arm. Zoe seemed delighted, and the smile on his daughter's face was all the thank-you he needed.

The doorbell rang, and Brian opened the door to Gerald and Dieter in their tuxes, with Dieter looking as though he were going to jump out of his skin with excitement. "Are you ready to go?" Gerald asked before motioning them outside. They slipped on their coats and followed Gerald down the steps. Zoe gasped and squealed when she saw the black limousine parked in their driveway, the driver holding the door open. The guys all waited for Nicolai to help Zoe inside before climbing into the large vehicle. The seats were plush and soft music was playing. Once they were moving, Gerald handed Zoe a small glass of soda before popping the cork on a bottle of Champagne. Pouring glasses, he handed one to each of the men.

They sipped and talked as they rode down the freeway. Zoe wanted to open the sun roof and stand through it like they did in the movies, but Brian put a stop to that. Looking to Nicolai, he stared into his lover's eyes, smiling to beat the band.

The ride took almost half an hour, but eventually they pulled up to the Milwaukee Art Museum entrance and got out of the car. Brian saw the driver hand Gerald a card for the ride home before closing the door behind them.

Brian couldn't help standing for a few seconds after the limo pulled away, looking up at the striking building shaped like a ship, complete with a retracting brise-soleil that looked like sails, the entire building bathed in light.

Inside the atrium, under the banks of skylights, the room glittered with elegant ladies in shimmering gowns and men in evening wear. Dieter and Gerald were met by someone from the museum who led them all to the front of the room, where a small platform had been constructed near the bank of windows that overlooked the lake and formed the bow of the ship. Dieter and the man from the museum stepped onto the platform and everyone quieted down. "Ladies and gentlemen, I'm Harvey Jenkins, the director of the museum, and I want to welcome all of you here this evening for the opening of an amazing exhibition. I'd like to thank the Friends of the Milwaukee Art Museum as well as Mr. Dieter Krumpf for making this exhibit possible. The story behind this exhibit is a fascinating one. I'm going to turn over the spotlight, as it were, to Mr. Krumpf so he can tell it to you in his own words. Mr. Dieter Krumpf." Those assembled applauded as Dieter stepped to the microphone. Brian noticed he looked nervous as he removed some papers from inside his jacket.

"Good evening, everyone, and thank you for coming," Dieter started to say, and Brian felt Nicolai move closer, his hand sliding into his. "*The Woman in Blue* was my great-grandmother, and from all accounts, she was quite a lady. The painting was commissioned as a gift to her husband, and even after she died, he held it dear to him, until World War II changed everything. When my great-grandfather, Joseph Meinauer, fled Austria ahead of the Nazis, he and my grandmother left everything behind except what they could carry." Brian knew the story, but found it fascinating, as did the rest of the room, because he could have heard a pin drop.

"*The Woman in Blue*, along with the rest of the Meinauer art collection, was scattered, with some of the pieces ending up in the Belvedere Museum, where they remained until very recently."

Dieter took a breath, and Brian could see him becoming more at ease as he went on. Brian looked at Nicolai and felt his lover squeeze his hand. Brian looked to his other side, expecting to see Zoe, but she wasn't there. Looking around, he saw her standing next to Uncle Gerald, holding his hand.

"Over three years ago, I began a quest, with the help of some people who would become my best friends, and one of them, my partner, to win the return of my family legacy. This quest took us to federal court and eventually the Supreme Court, and ended in a ruling in our favor." Dieter paused for a few seconds. "Now, like many of you, I thought that would be the end, but it wasn't, because all we'd won legally was the right to sue here in the United States. But we had also frightened the Austrian government, and they offered a deal. They agreed to set up a commission to examine the case, hear our evidence, and rule definitively on the ownership of *The Woman in Blue* as well as the four Pirktl landscapes that you will see tonight. I talked at length with my partner Gerald, my attorney Brian, as well as his partner and my dear friend, Nicolai."

When Brian heard that, he turned and saw Nicolai's tear-filled eyes, and he squeezed his hand before moving closer and placing his arm around Nicolai's waist.

"We knew we were taking a chance, but the alternative was more years of lengthy and costly litigation, so we accepted. Three retired Austrian judges heard out our case, and I have to tell you, I expected them to only rule partially in our favor and come up with a monetary payment so the paintings could remain in Austria. I would not have been happy, but that was what I expected. Instead, the judges ruled unanimously that the paintings did indeed belong to the Meinauer family and should be returned." Dieter paused again, and Brian could feel the tension in the room. "I was actually asked at an interview I did a few months ago why I didn't donate the paintings back to the museum, and I told them that the Belvedere had had *The Woman in Blue* for almost seventy-five years and that was long enough." Brian heard a collective chuckle ripple through the room. "So this evening, I'd like to welcome all of you to the exhibit of the reconstructed Meinauer collection, entitled, *Recovering Looted Nazi Art.*"

The crowd applauded, and the doors to the exhibit opened. The crowd began to mill around as the first people entered the exhibit. Brian still held Nicolai's hand as they made their way to where Dieter, Gerald, and Zoe were talking to people as they filtered in.

"This is amazing," Brian told Dieter. "I'm so glad we were able help work this out." Once Dieter had been awarded the paintings, other issues had presented themselves. As much as Dieter wanted to hang the paintings in his and Gerald's home, it wasn't practical for many reasons, the least of which was security. There were also sizable legal bills that had to be paid. Granted, Brian had done what he could to minimize them, but the lawsuit had been expensive.

"It was your idea, and you did more than anyone to make it happen," Dieter said before hugging Brian. "The idea of leasing the Pirktls to the museum for ten years was brilliant. I still own them, and the museum gets an artistic draw that it would never get otherwise."

"I'm pretty proud myself, and I'm especially pleased they were able to come up with the money. Your legal bills have been paid, and your family legacy has been returned. I think this is a happy ending."

To Brian's surprise, Dieter shook his head. "It's almost a happy ending. Come on, let's go see the exhibit."

Brian wondered what Dieter meant, but let Zoe walk ahead as they entered the space. A permanent exhibit space had been developed as part of the deal. Nicolai and Dieter had worked with the museum staff using the pictures in Dieter's photo album as well as pictures they'd taken on their trip to Vienna to recreate the room in Dieter's great-grandparents' home where *The Woman in Blue* and the four Pirktl landscapes had originally hung, down to the furniture and lighting. The other works that had been returned, including Brian and Nicolai's Dürer woodcuts, hung in adjacent galleries.

The five of them entered the recreated Viennese salon and looked around the room. In this setting and lighting, the paintings appeared much more powerful. Shadows played over the landscape canvases, making the movement in the trees seem more pronounced. Dieter was asked to stand next to the portrait of his great-grandmother as a few people took pictures. Then he stepped back and let other people look.

"This is the happy ending, Brian. We, the five of us, are the happy ending." Dieter lifted Zoe into his arms and hugged her.

"I don't understand," Brian said as he signed what Dieter had said for Nicolai.

Dieter stood where he could see his great-grandmother's portrait. "*The Woman in Blue* was painted as a gift from Anna to Joseph because she loved him. Yes, Anna was beautiful, but I think some of her love for Joseph comes through in the portrait."

Brian wasn't sure where Dieter was going with this, but he signed what Dieter said, and listened.

"When I started this whole case, I only wanted the return of my family legacy, mostly as a memorial to Gram, but what I really found was Gerald. And when he turned the case over to Brian, Brian found Nicolai. So I've come to believe that *The Woman in Blue* is sort of magical. She came to be because of Anna's love for Joseph, and she brought the four of us love as well. I think that's the real happy ending to the story." Dieter set Zoe on her feet, and Gerald placed an arm around Dieter's waist, and Brian felt Nicolai's hand on his back. Together the five of them wandered through the gallery looking at the collection of artworks. Brian noticed that Dieter stopped in front of the small portrait of his grandmother, and he wondered if he said anything to her, but he didn't ask.

At the end of the evening, after seeing the rest of the museum, Brian and Nicolai stood in front of *The Woman in Blue* while the others saw the last of what they wanted to see. "I think Dieter is right—you can see the love in her expression," Nicolai signed to Brian, "and maybe she is magical."

"Maybe," Brian agreed. "After all, in a way, she brought me you, and I'll believe in magic or just about anything else if it means I get to have you in my life." Brian stopped signing and moved close to Nicolai, feeling the heat from his body through his tux. He had found love, and as he stood with Nicolai, Brian said a silent thank-you to Anna, the woman in blue.

ANDREW GREY grew up in western Michigan with a father who loved to tell stories and a mother who loved to read them. Since then he has lived throughout the country and traveled throughout the world. He has a master's degree from the University of Wisconsin-Milwaukee and works in information systems for a large corporation. Andrew's hobbies include collecting antiques, gardening, and leaving his dirty dishes anywhere but in the sink (particularly when writing). He considers himself blessed with an accepting family, fantastic friends, and the world's most supportive and loving partner. Andrew currently lives in beautiful historic Carlisle, Pennsylvania.

Visit Andrew's web site at http://www.andrewgreybooks.com and blog at http://andrewgreybooks.livejournal.com/. E-mail him at andrewgrey @comcast.net.

Contemporary Romance by ANDREW GREY

Also by ANDREW GREY

http://www.dreamspinnerpress.com

Contemporary Romance by ANDREW GREY

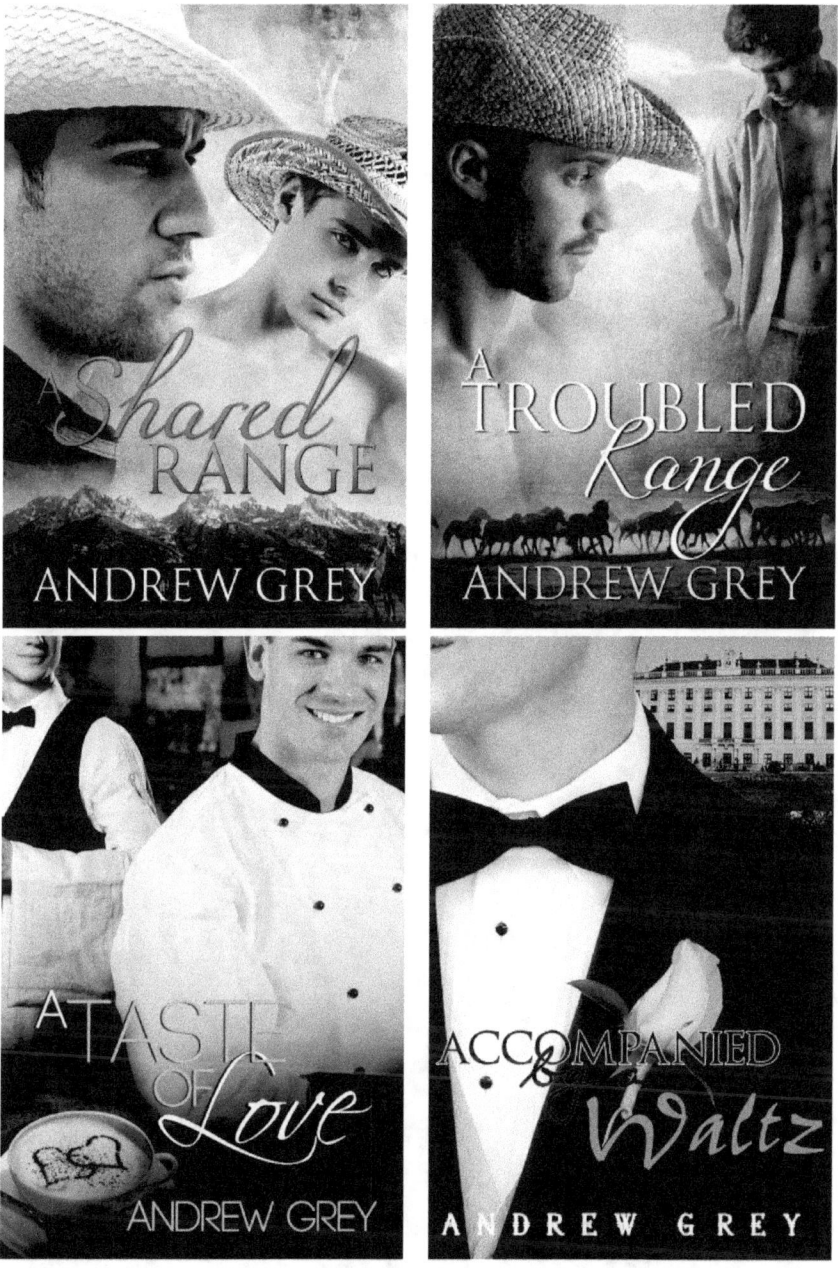

Contemporary Fantasy by ANDREW GREY

www.ingramcontent.com/pod-product-compliance
Lightning Source LLC
Chambersburg PA
CBHW070017260626
47159CB00005B/1842